A Family Divided by Color

A Novel By

Amanda Lee

Vicious Ink Publications

The characters, events, and circumstances in this story are entirely fictional. Any resemblances to any person who is living or dead, place or event are merely coincidental.
Amanda Manning
 Publisher

Vicious Ink Publications
4209 Lakeland Dr., Ste, 329
Flowood, MS 39232
www.viciousinkpublications.com
vipsubmissions@gmail.com

Thank you for your support!

Amanda Lee

5/14/13

Introduction

There are things about a person that you can see but what you cannot see could have a profound effect upon one's existence. Consequently, we are unable to see the outward features and actions of people and not the inward; however, it is what we cannot see that may affect racial existence.

In many cases, what we cannot see are struggles with personal racism. With a solemn mind, we love our families and ourselves but drunkenness causes our eyes to be clouded with racism and separatism; therefore, we act indifferent and judgmental towards others.

Strangely enough, the appearance and reality become the same. Value is not determined by that which is seen, for racism gives rise to race not the other way around. A simple thing called 'skin pigment' can destroy the existence of a family. This thought imposes the face about how far will a woman go to protect your child?

Abby had no limitations when it came to her children. She knew all too well how painful the world they lived in could cave in and cause her child to question his very own existence. As much as she tried to shield her children from hate, she knew she could only do so much.

True mothers have an instinct that naturally protects their children from situations inflicted by society. Although, racial divisions exist in families, it is love that surpasses all understanding. The world can be very cruel and ugly.

Chapter 1

Abby Brenner lived in a rundown house with her two sons because it was the only place they could afford to stay. She could have lived with her parents, but her father hated her son, and, of course, he hated her because she had a son by a White man. Abby's father, John, disliked White people, but Abby didn't care about color. To her, it was all about how a person treated you and not the color of their skin. Her father came from a time of the fifties and sixties when racism was a big issue. White people hated Black people, and Black people hated White people. But, it was 2000, and Abby felt he should leave that mess in the past.

Abby struggled while she took care of her sons. She had been beaten like a dog, treated like a slave, but nothing could compare to losing her son. She prayed and prayed to God to hold her family together as one while she worked part-time at a grocery store and took hand me down clothes and shoes for her kids. Abby depended on welfare to help support her sons and she hated to struggle but was sure God would make a way. Abby was twenty-seven with two sons, Peter was twelve and Alex was ten.

Her struggles were difficult because she ran from shelter to shelter because of the lights being turned off to not having enough food to feed her kids. Abby worked part-time at a grocery store to keep food on the table. There were many nights when she went to bed hungry, but she made sure Peter and Alex was full. After all her struggles, she never gave up hope that God would find a way. Prayer was the best solution. After being criticized by her father for so many years, Abby built up enough courage to do better with her life.

Abby Brenner thought of what racism and hate brought to her family as a memory flashed by of when she first got pregnant with Peter. With her head hung low, sorrow on her chest and a baby growing in her stomach Abby Brenner sat in the park discouraged. For the second time in her life she felt alone and believed she had nowhere to go but up. She had to strive to make it to where she was in her life and she worried as she pat her stomach and faintly smiled. "What would I do if Joseph turned his back on me, too?" she thought with agony.

Her lips began to quiver and her eyes became full of tears, all alone and desperate she cried. No matter how much she wiped the tears flowed everywhere, none stop. Abby loved Joseph and believed he loved her so, but many obstacles stood in their way. His father did not believe in mixing of the races and her family mostly her father didn't either. The more she thought on her situation the more tears fell. *How am I to tell my heart who to love or not too because of family skin differences?* Abby thought with her mind as pain filled her heart. She lifted her head to see if anyone paid any attention to her and for the most they didn't; therefore, she wiped her eyes some and took into account that the sun was still shined, no matter how horrible she felt, birds sung, even if she wanted to hear them or not, and everything around her flowed in perfect harmony. *If only my life was like that*, she thought as she sat on the bench with a heavy heart and weary feelings.

Into her vision young mothers played with their children and some people walked their dogs, but she could not focus, her mind was in a faraway place and her life too far gone to go back. With her hormones racing and feelings of inferiority she cried more and more. *What am I going to do? I already have one son whose father is a dead beat dad and now pregnant by another man who has everything.* Abby could not stop the tears as they escaladed down her face like a river breaking. She hung her head again and remembered too well how her parents felt about her spending too much time working with Joseph or the enemy as they would call him, but she had grown to love him and knows that he loves her, too, but racial differences divided them, even though its only skin deep.

For the first time since she sat on the bench it had just occurred to her that life goes on, in spite of how she felt and thought. She has to continue on not only would she have one son but two that would count on her for support, love, and protection from the evil this world has to offer.

All Abby could think about was the hate and racism her son might face once he came into this world. The rejection from his father would definitely be a disaster. How did she fall so deep in fall in love with a White man?

Chapter 2

Finally Peter got up the nerves to talk to his father. He didn't believe that his father didn't want him. What if his father did beat his mother near death? So What? There is no way a father would deny his only son. Peter thought to himself, *how could he not love me?* Peter knew his father hated him because he was half Black. It was not his fault, but he was the blame because he was born. The loneliness was unbearable. The heart break of his mother's father not loving him. That man hated him with a passion. The rest of the family tolerated him because he belongs to Abby. He can't help the fact his father is White. The kids at school picked at him calling him racial slurs. Peter attended an all-Black school and the children bullied him every day. He hated his life and wanted change. He was going to keep going until he made a change in his life even if it meant leaving his mother behind.

Peter left home early that Saturday morning. His mother and Alex were back home sleep. It was the day that he decided if he wanted to be with his father or not. He loved his mother, but he wanted his father's love more.

Peter walked up to a big office building designed with dark glass. He pulled on the door, but it was locked. Suddenly, a man pushed the door open and there stood his father, Joseph. His mouth dropped. He couldn't speak.

"What is it boy?" Joseph asked sternly.

"I would like to speak with you."

"Does your mother know that you are down here?"

"No, she doesn't. Do you know who I am?"

"Of course, Peter."

Joseph stared at Peter for a few moments admiring his seed. Peter looked exactly like him when he was a young boy. He wanted dearly to love his son, but that Black side of him would ruin him for sure. Joseph felt like all Blacks were ignorant. His heart began to melt, but then the image of those Black men beating him near death flashed before his eyes. That night he tried to fight for his life, but lost the battle. Abby's father wanted him dead. He vows to never love another Black woman again or get involved with any Black people unless it was necessary. He hated Black people with a passion just as much as Abby's father hated White people.

Joseph grabbed Peter by the shirt and pulled him into the building. He held Peter's shirt until they reached his office. He swung him around and sat him down hard into a wooden chair.

"What the hell do you want? Why are you here?"

"I want to know why you hate me. Why you don't want me," Peter asked angrily.

"Boy is that why you are here. Go home," Joseph shouted and he snatched Peter up by his shirt and threw him out his office door. Peter fell to the floor hard as he looked up at his father. He jumped up and ran off.

"Peter, wait," Joseph shouted.

He ran until he got to the front door. Peter stopped and looked back. Joseph came behind him. Joseph stopped behind Peter and put his hand on his shoulder.

"Peter, I can't be with you until you decide to leave them people."

"What people?" Peter asked while he pulled at his ear.

"Those niggas you live with. You will never succeed as long as you are with them. Look how you live and how you dress. When you leave, you must never return."

"You mean I have to leave mother?"

"Screw your mother. Like I said, when you decide to leave then call me. Until then, get your ass out of here," Joseph screamed as he shoved Peter out the door.

Peter turned and looked at Joseph as he spoke, "But why?"

"Those niggas caused me a lot of pain and suffering."

"Joseph, stop calling them that."

"That's what they are. I see you are not ready to live with me."

"Yes, I'm ready. Please father I love you."

Joseph looked at Peter. Those words kind of bothered him. He really didn't want to have anything to do with this kid, but he was his son.

"Come back in. I need to explain myself."

Peter walked back in the building. Joseph closed the door and just looked at Peter.

"When your mother was pregnant with you, her father and uncles beat me near death. Everyone thought it was my father that beat me for getting a Black girl pregnant. They could have killed me. I loved Abby, but after that I vowed to never, ever like another Black person again. All those niggas are the same."

"Did mother know what happened?"

"No, but I put that same ass whipping on her. She will never forget that. I tried to kill her, but I couldn't."

"Kill her?"

"Yes boy, that's what I said. I can't love you. You are Black and you will always be Black. I just want no part of your life."

"I'm half White. I look more White not Black. Do you know how bad my life is with kids always beating me up and picking on me? Please don't do this to me. I want to come live with you."

"I can't. Just go on and get out of here boy."

Peter stood there with tears running down his face. He began to cry and Joseph grabbed him by his shirt. He opened the door and shoved Peter out onto the ground. He fell on the ground and then he scrapped his elbow. Joseph shut the door in his face and locked it. Peter was so hurt because he thought his father would embrace him and love him. But, he had to make a decision. In order for him to win his father's love, he had to get rid of his mother. She had to be gone from his life completely. He loved his mother, but his father's love was what he desired. That day, Peter decided to get his mother out of his life for good.

Peter took off running until he got to the edge of some woods. He ran as far as he could then fell to the ground crying. He spoke, "God why are you punishing me like this? My father hates me; my mother looks at me with hate in her eyes. Both sides of my family are filled with hate. Why? I just want to be loved. Please, God, I don't want this life anymore. Please, take me away." Peter continued to lay on the ground for nearly an hour. His mind was made up. As soon as he graduates from high school and move off to college, he vowed to never return. He loved his mother and brother, Alex, but he loved Joseph more. He desired for so long to belong, but nobody accepted him.

Back at the office, Joseph stared out the huge window as he watched Peter run away crying. Tears fell down his face because he wanted so much to love him, but that mother of his ruined it. He couldn't believe that he was once in love with a Black woman. Blacks were all the same. His family taught him that Blacks were made to work in the cotton fields. He should have kept Abby as that, *a house nigga*.

Joseph's thoughts continued as he began to think about his horrible experience in the hospital. A machine breathed for him as a long transparent tube came out of his throat and a green tube in his stomach; however, large bags of morphine dripped into his left hand IV and bigger bags of blood were draining fast into Joseph's right hand IV. His arms and legs seem to dangle as they were in slings while bandages covered him almost completely. His face was full of cuts, swollen, purple and blue. As for his eyes they were closed tightly and for what she could see trails of tears marked the side of his face. Joseph was unconscious and looked to be in so much pain.

He could hear his father say, "Haven't you people done enough to my son? He loved you and this is the payment he gets for loving a damn nigga? My son could die and if he does not come out of this you and your people will pay. Do you hear me? Leave and do not ever show your face again. If you do I will have your Black ass arrested and those sons of yours in the system where he will end up anyway. As for your bastard child, it is not welcomed here as long as I have breath in my body. Joseph knew he was talking to Abby. He had a tear to roll down his face. He was devastated by the entire situation.

Abby couldn't help but cry. Deep down inside she knew that Joseph's father was right. She loved him so much that she was willing to let go. How could she put Joseph through this pain and humiliation?

Chapter 3

Alex and Peter lay down in bed and talked. Alex was on the top bunk and Peter was on the bottom, and they had the window open, as they listened to the crickets sound out as the moon shone bright.

"Look at the moon, it shines so bright," Peter spoke.

"It does. I wonder if it shines like that all over the world," Alex remarked.

"Of course it does."

"How do you know?"

"It does," Peter replied as a matter of fact.

Alex sighed to himself.

"What's the matter with you?" Peter asked.

"I hate this raggedy house. I wish I was living in New York or Hollywood being a famous movie star."

"Don't forget about me. I want to be famous, too, one day," Peters said as he grabbed his sketch book and colored pencils from under his bed and began to draw.

He lay on his stomach while his feet

swung from side to side. Peter pulled out a small flashlight from under his pillow for more light to draw.

"What you doing, drawing again?" Alex asked as he took out a Hershey candy bar from under his pillow. He opened it and bit down on it as he shook his head from side to side, staring at it.

"I have a secret, but you better not tell."

"A secret? Why are you keeping secrets?"

"Just promise me you won't tell mama or anybody."

"I promise." Alex looked down over the rail at Peter.

"Well out with it, because if you keep it on the inside, it'll only tear you up so I'm listening," Alex continued.

Peter waits a few minutes to gather his thoughts. Then finally, with a low tone he states, "I wish mother was White."

"You what?"

"With an even louder tone because the first time he said it he couldn't believe he was actually said that out loud, "I wish mother was White."
Alex looked like the blood was drained from his face and he gradually said, "Why do you

want that?"

"I see how well my father dressed, I see the car he drives, and it doesn't look like he's struggling like we are.

"I understand that, but he doesn't love you like mama does."

"What's love when you have money? You don't see the way she looks at me."

"Is that what's important to you, money? Mama looks at you no different than me."

"How can you say that, Alex? You don't know how it feels to be a third wheel in this house. I'm half White, half Black. You are all Black. I'm confused about which race to be called. I know you see no difference besides the fact I'm your brother."

"So you are saying you don't think mama love you?"

"I know mama loves me, but I don't feel it. She probably wishes I was never born. Maybe she just treats me like she loves me. Sometimes she treats me like I'm invisible. Like for instance, when we go to the store she buy you things then remember that I'm with her and then she'll let me get something. Just face it, she loves you more than me."

"Stop talking about her like that.

Mama isn't like that and you know that for a fact she treats us equally so why are you being ignorant."

"Reality is that she loves you more Alex. I wish one day that my father comes and take me away from this dump. I hate it here. You don't love me either, so why pretend."

"Peter, you know that's not true. I will go tell mother and ask her to tell you how she feels. I love you Peter and no matter what u say, think or do will change my mind of how much I love you."

"Please, you don't love me."

Alex face went from a smile to a frown in seconds. He lay back on his bed and rolled his eyes. Peter threw down his sketch book and pencils. Alex was surprised at Peter. He had hurt on his face, but he got into bed, lay on his side, and closed his eyes. Alex thought *why my brother is acting like this. Ever since he saw Joseph it seems like he's a different person. I don't have my father in my life either and don't care if he's dead or alive. That's not going to make me turn my back on my mother just because of the color of our skin. Peter has had trouble with kids, but I always had his back. Always and now this. My thoughts were to turn my back on him and leave him alone, but I can't do it. Mama's father hates Peter, Joseph's entire family hates him. Mama and I are all he's got.*

For the first time Alex looked at his brother as if he was a stranger because the things he spoke didn't make sense to him at all and he felt like he protected a mere shadow of a brother.

Peter lay in bed and his thoughts were of Joseph that day he went to visit him. "Hi Peter, my son. Come in and join me," Joseph spoke.

"Yes father," Peter replied with a big Kool-Aid smile.

"I've waiting on you to come to me. It's time for me to take you away from all this drama. Are you ready to live with me?"

"Yes father. Please don't make me go back to those niggas. I hate them all. We belong together as a family."

"Son, those niggas are going to be the death of you. I don't see how you have stayed so long with them," Joseph spoke as he lit one of his Cuban cigars.

"Does it bother you that I'm part Black?" Peter tossed that question out there.

"You're right. I can't love you. You're a nigga. You're one of them," Joseph yelled out loud and began to laugh until tears were coming down his face.

"Father no. I'm not one of them. Please accept me. I'm not one of them," Peter yelled as he realized and snapped back to reality that it wasn't real.

Peter turned on his side looking out the window. He wondered why God punished him.

Chapter 4

Early the next morning, Peter woke up to the smell of bacon and eggs. He looked at the big army watch on his wrist and it read five thirty, which was too early for his mother to be cooking. She usually started breakfast around six or six thirty. He got up and headed to the bathroom, brushed his teeth and washed his face. He then walked to the kitchen as he rubbed his eyes. Peter stood behind their mother brushing her hair. She sat down with a pink floral robe that they bought for Mother's Day.

"Hey sleepy head. Did we wake you?" Abby asked.

"I smelled bacon."

"Is that all you smelled? No eggs or grits?" she stated as she got up from the table and placed a kiss on his forehead.

Peter sat down at the table and stared at Alex, who stared back at him. The two boys looked as if they would fight right then and there.

"You two need to wash your hands or use some of that hand sanitizer."
They both grabbed the bottle, but Alex

snatched it out of Peter's hand. Abby looked at the two boys as they stared at each other down.

"Are you two boys alright?"

"Peter has a secret to tell."

"Shut up," Peter snapped.

"What secret?" Abby asked while she stood at the stove to fix the boys' plates.

"Peter, tell Mama your secret."

"I told you to shut up," Peter said as he picked up a bowl of salt and threw it in Alex's face. Alex yelled while he held his hands to his face, and then he fell to the floor as he kicked and screamed. Abby picked him up off the floor and rushed him over to the sink to wash his face. Alex tossed water on his eyes as he moaned. Peter stood back and he looked evil.

"What's gotten into you?" Abby yelled.

Peter stood there firmly. He was pissed off and ready to kill Alex because he didn't want his secret out.

"Answer me!"

"Why do you hate me so much? I see the way you look at me. Why you hate me?" Peter screamed.

"Hate you? Are you crazy? You are my son and I love you."

"Stop lying! I hate you! I hate you! I hate you!"

"Peter."

Peter ran over to Abby and swung at her. He hit Abby in the arm before she caught his hands to try to hold him down. Then, she grabbed him around the waist with his arms at his side and held him very tight.

"Peter, stop it!"

"I hate you! I hate you! I hate you!" Peter continued to scream.

Peter yelled and screamed until him and Abby went down to the floor. Abby sat on the floor and she held Peter down as he bucked and kicked. She held on tightly to him because she didn't know why he doubted her love. Alex stood there as he watched the two of them.

Abby rocked Peter like a baby. She hummed until he stopped crying. When he calmed down, Abby spoke.

"I love you so much, Peter. Stop doubting my love for you. You are my son. My flesh and blood. I will always love you," she held his face in her hands.

Peter had tears streaming down his face. "I love you, too, mama, but why do you look at me sometimes as if you don't want me?"

"Peter, I want you. I love you," she spoke softly.

Peter looked into his mother's eyes and put his arms around her, then held her tightly. She looked at Alex as he still had an evil glare on his face. She thought about all this drama and never found out what the secret was really about. She wanted to know what really set Peter off. All she ever tried to do was protect her family. It failed her once but never again as her thoughts went back to when DHS took her kids away. They all got out and walked toward the mall entrance. Peter passed a security guard and looked at him in a frightening way. The security guard looked at the trio and stared closely at Peter, but continued on his rounds. Alex led them to a store and inside where people Peter knew. He ducked behind some clothing and hid but his White classmates saw him and came over to him.

"What you doing?" One of his classmates asked.

"I am just looking" Peter said as he made sure his family was not around.

He didn't see Abby come behind him, but out of the blue she came over to him and said, "I didn't know you had friends."

The boys looked puzzled at Peter and

he could have died right then, but instead the first thing to come to his mind was, "I don't know you crazy lady, get away from me."

Abby was speechless at first but she spoke, "Peter what are you talking about?"

Peter and the boys took out running towards the security guard he made eye contact with earlier.

"What's wrong son?" he asked.

"That Black lady kidnapped me!" he screamed.

People stared and as the security guard went over to Abby. He got on the portable walkie talkie and called dispatcher for police. She kept trying to prove to them that he was her son, but none believed her because he presented himself as a White boy kidnapped by a Black woman.

The police arrived and arrested Abby. She was pissed at Peter, but he acted like he was afraid. In truth he was because he knew he had messed up by lying, but that was the only thing he could think of, but he regretted lying.

They took Alex and Peter to a state funded boy's shelter and called DHS. Abby was charged with kidnapping and disorderly conduct. It took a week before they found out that Peter was lying. All charges against her were dropped but the boys could not return to her just yet. *Thank God the home is in better shape*, she thought as DHS had to come see where she lived before her sons could be returned to her.

Abby was not angry with Peter, she was more disappointed than anything. *How can my son be so angry with me*? She thought as she lay in her house alone for the first time in years. The more she tossed and turned her mind allowed her to be awaken with the question she needed an answer to, which was why was he denying her?

The boys stayed in the system for three weeks. Alex was angry at Peter, but he liked the nice room and food; therefore, he didn't complain. Peter on the other hand was scared because there were a lot of other Black boys his age there. Majority of the people around him were nice, but many were mean to him and that only increased his dislikes for his mother's heritage.

On the court date Abby saw her boys and she hugged and squeezed them both, for she truly missed them. They were equally happy to see her. The judge ordered them to therapy because he believed that Peter had issues with being who he was and why he was the way he was. She was ordered to take the boys to therapy the following morning and if she didn't obey she would be in jail and the boys back into the system.

When they arrived home, Abby had ice cream and cake for them to celebrate their reunion.

"Peter I am not angry with you. I love you and I always will. We can change who we are on the outside, but it is the inside that stays the same," Abby said.

"One day, can we go to Mega Fun Time, just the three of us?" Peter asked because he always liked the rides he saw there.

"When we can I will take you both," Abby replied as she looked up in the rear view mirror at her son. She couldn't believe this was the same son who just accused her of kidnapping him a few weeks ago.

The next morning they all arrived at the therapist. After that day they all did a number of sessions on abandonment issues of the absent fathers. After attending therapy for over six months Abby thought her sons did better, but on the particular last day of counseling Abby's world again caved in. Alex did fine with coping with how things happened in his life. He knew his dad was in jail for selling drugs near a school, buying alcohol for minor girls and strong arm robbery; however, he cared not that he would see his father or his father's family because to him, they didn't deserve his love or his time. The only thing that mattered was those in his household and mainly his brother because he loved him even if Peter did not love him as much.

Peter sat on the side of his mother while Alex had to wait in the hall. He didn't look like an average boy his age. He was very clean and nothing was out of place. Peter's hair was blond and curly with a hint of underlying Black curl or two. His posture was straight as a board and his answers were short and blunt, with no regard to who got hurt. His grades where excellent and he always went out and beyond to achieve higher than anyone in his class. His problem was misdirected blame, which went towards his mother.

"Peter today is the last day of counseling, how do you feel?" the Psychiatrist asked.

"I am well, thank you, but still I do not understand why I am here?" He said again.

"You told a security guard that you were kidnapped by your biological mother,"

The Psychiatrist stated.

"We can sit here all day and waste money that could be easily spent on helping others that need it, but I will say this, I don't know who my dad is and I do not understand why I am White in a Black household and how my momma treats me and Alex different." Abby turned and look at her son, whom was sitting next to her without flinching or biting his tongue.

"Ms. Brennan," The Psychiatrist said "How do you feel about your son stating that you treat your sons different?"

"If anything, ever since my father told Peter of his color, he has been not easy to help. I try to shield them from hatred people have to show. I believe Peter needs more love and attention than Alex does and that is probably why he knows that I tend to his needs a lot more, for he is fragile and easily hurt, than Alex."

The Psychiatrist says, "Do you blame your mother for something she had no control over?"

He looks at his mother and says, "I believe it is her fault that I am poor Black trash. People look at me like I am sick. Even your parents look at me funny and pay me not any attention like they do Alex. Then I look at you both and think maybe they are right."

"No baby, they are not right. People look at your skin tone and judge you from there because that is all they see," Abby sincerely spoke with tears in her eyes.

"When I get older I am going to find my father and live with him, so I can feel important."

"Peter focus back to me," The Psychiatrist said.

"Do you love your mother and your brother?" the Psychiatrist asked.

"As for my mom, she is trying, but I really don't know. I suppose to, but a part of me won't let me. As for my brother, I do I just wish his dad was White so we could hang out more and be closer," Peter said as he looked away from her.

When Abby heard that she wanted to die. For all the years of Peter's life she shielded him from bigotry and hate. It was true he looked White all over and if you didn't know him you would not know he was mixed at all. All the years of him not wanting to talk to her family was not because of being a shy child, it was because he hated the part of him she gave him, his heritage and his color. She knew that their healing must begin because she could see that she was losing her son to color and that wasn't fair. He acted more and more like the people she tried to keep away from him. *Thankfully Alex could not hear of this*, she thought.

Right then and there she decided to tell her son the truth about everything so they would understand how color destroyed her life and if he wasn't careful it could shatter his existence.

She looks at Peter and says, "I am going to be frank with you and tell you now, what has happened. Your father loved me and I loved him. When I got pregnant with you we drifted apart. His family wouldn't allow you to be in their lives."

Peter looked at her and started crying. She leaned his head on her shoulder and spoke on "Our families did not approve of us being grown and in love. When they almost killed him your father, your grandfather told me to leave and never return. After I had you, I went to see your father and as bad as he was hurt he managed to tell me that he hated me and my kind. I thought my life ended, but when I look at you and your brother, I no longer feel that way. We got evicted and moved here. I haven't heard or seen your father since then. His father made it clear to me that you were not welcomed and neither was your Black DNA."

Peter stopped crying and listened with dismay and yet he still blamed his mother, even though, the blame was not entirely her fault something would not let him let go of anger he felt for her. That day he vowed he would find his father and be with his. White DNA. Black DNA. He didn't care. He would make his father love him.

Chapter 5

The sun was hot and muggy. Abby, Peter, and Alex had worked in the garden. She was very dirty and sweaty. The boys stopped working, and then they played and ran around in circles. Abby took a drink of water from an old milk jug. Her body had to rest because her hands were blistered and body felt very tired. Then she watched the boys play.

Suddenly, Peter stopped in his tracks. He looked as if he had seen a ghost. Alex ran over to see what he was looking at.

"What you doing?" Alex yelled out.

Alex stopped and stared at the ground, and then Abby began to wonder what they saw. She walked toward the boys as they looked down at the ground. The boys stood there as they stared at a big snake. Peter began to sweat and tears fell down his face.

Alex grabbed Peter's hand and said, "I'll protect you."

The snake rose up to strike, but Alex pushed Peter out of the way from harm. Peter fell to the ground and Alex jumped. The snake struck Alex on the side of his face and rushed off into the garden. Alex yelled and screamed as Peter stood there frozen solid. Abby rushed over to the boys, but fell down before she got to Alex. She began to crawl up to him and observed two small snake bites to the face. Abby struggled to pick up Alex and rushed off to the car. She opened the back door of the car and lay Alex down, then hopped into the car, turned the ignition, and then she backed up. Suddenly, she realized that Peter still stood there frozen.

"Peter. Peter, come on," Abby yelled out as tears streamed down her face.

He didn't move. He stood there in space. Abby had to jump out of the car and run over to him. She was in a panic because she never thought to check on him to see if the snake bit him, too. Abby was scared to death. She rushed up to him and shook him. "Are you alright? Did the snake bite you?"

"No, mother," he stated.

She grabbed Peter's hand and rush off to the car as Alex yelled louder for her. They got to the car, Peter jumped in the front seat, and then she looked back at Alex, and Abby headed for the hospital.

As she drove faster and faster, her mind raced back to the incident with her father speaking ignorant to her son. Abby looked over at Peter as his eyes was looking straight ahead not flinching at all. Her father words hurt so badly. "Look at you boy, you are White, looking just like your sorry daddy. He's not fit for the skin he's in."

Peter stopped drawing and asked "What is White?"
He looked down at Peter and smiled because he now has the opportunity to tell him what he thinks. He looked up to see if anyone was around and they were all in the house. He said in a very mean way, "Come here boy."

Being obedient he put the book on the step and he stood in front of his grandfather. "Stick out your hand," he said as he extended his and Peter as well.
"Anything darker than you is Black. Yo kind of people has more money than me. Y'all have everything and Blacks are struggling. We work hard to get what we want unlike you Whites. Everything is given to you on a silver splatter."

"Silver Splatter?" Peter said trying to understand what is being said to him.

"Boy not only is you White, you dumb and you slow. Look at yo mom? She Black. Look at your brother, he Black. Look at how y'all live down there? Holes everywhere, clothes don't look clean, run down house, no running water, yo poor, no money and pitiful. Yo momma had a great job until you came along. She was going to be somebody, but no that White father of yours messed her life by giving her you. Why did you have to come along and mess up our lives? She should have aborted you."

"Abort me?" Peter says still confused.

"Didn't you hear me, boy? She should have flushed you down the toilet?"

"Down the toilet?" Peter said still not understanding the conversation.

"White people have it all, but you are poor Black nigga thrash."

"You mean because I am White I am better and I am nothing because I am with back people?" Peter said as he sounded confused more than ever.

"Boy you need to go to sped. You don't understand anything I'm telling you," Abby's father said sounding angrier than before.

"I understand everything you're saying to me," Peter spoke while looking angry.

"That's right boy, do us a favor, leave and don't ever come back. You are a pathetic and not worth the dirt you standing on."

A Family Divided by Color

Peter looked down at the ground then back up to his grandfather's face and replied, "I'm not worth dirt?" Peter looked down again and saw all kinds of trash on the ground. It didn't look pretty in his eyes, in fact it was nasty and some of it stunk to his nose.

"Boy if you were worth anything people wouldn't look at you when you are with Black people, now would they?"

"People look at me different because I am White?" Peter said as his breathing increased.

"Yeah boy, honestly I wish you were Black or never born, get away from me I can't stand you. The only reason she puts up with you because she had you. Poor Alex he has to play with a dirty White boy." Abby's father remarked with so much anger.

Small as Peter was he couldn't help but cry because now his eyes were open to race, color and hatred for Black people. Alex heard everything and it made him mad as he ran to the kitchen where his momma and grandma was.

"Mama!" Alex yelled.

Abby and her mother jumped up from the kitchen table, "What's wrong?"

"Grandpa told Peter he is pathetic and

not worth the dirt he stood on. He told him he is White and should deserve better than to be with Blacks like us," Alex repeated. Abby and her mother ran outside where her father was.

"You are not welcomed here for as long as I walk on this earth!" Abby said in a high angered voice as her father walked off the porch.

"John!" her mother said, "Why did you do that for? He is just a young child that sees the world like everyone is the same color? He doesn't know any better. That's your grandchild."

"As for being not welcome," he looked around and said "To what this piece of dump you call home? Somebody needed to tell the boy about his true color and if no one did he is soon to find out sooner are later."

"Abby, I am so sorry for your father's behavior. Go find your son and show him so much love and that color do not matter as long as you love him and take care of him," Her mother said as she fussed at her husband all the way to the truck.

Abby ran to find Peter and when she did he was next door and covered in Black smut with traces of water coming from his eyes.

A Family Divided by Color

"Mommy, I'm something now," Peter said as he dropped his head and cried.

She ran to her son and spoke, "You have always been some one. It doesn't matter what you look like. I love you. Your brother loves you and most importantly God loves you."

"Grandpa doesn't, he said ugly things to me and how I should be better than you and Blacks because I am White," he said.

"Baby, there are many people out there just like your grandpa. They can't see pass your color. They are mean and evil just like your grandpa," Abby explained as she held Peter and cried.

"Does being Black means we don't have money or a nice house?" Peter asked as he thought back to the things he just heard.

"No baby. It just means I need to find a job and do better by you both. Skin color is not all the issue and as for your grandpa he is not worth a stick in the mud."

Abby had never felt hatred before, but she discovered it aimed today towards her own father. She had to pray so that spirit would remove from her. Ever since her son was born she shielded him from her father and others like him. She didn't want him to feel that being Black was a curse or anything in that nature. Today her father's evil spirit showed up and hurt her son in such a way she didn't think he would ever forget but pray she would.

Chapter 6

When Peter walked into the classroom the next day, a bunch of Black boys stood in his way. Each time he moved one of them stepped in his face. Then, another one until he politely spoke, "Excuse yourself from my walkway, I need to get to class."

The taller of the boys turned around and saw Peter. The other boys made a semi-circle as the listen to their leader say, "Well if it isn't Mister I Don't Wanna Be Black. Why don't you go the other way around to your desk?"

Peter sighed and responded, "Why don't you learn your work so you can pass this class? My bad you are Black and you're dumb."

"If I'm so dumb then why do you have a White daddy and a Black mama? Seems like somebody in your family was dumb to have a baby by a cracker," the boy remarked and the other boys laughed.

"It does not fade me about what you say about them. One's a nigga and the other is a cracker. I don't care. Now, get out of my way," Peter demanded.

"You ain't nothing but a punk anyway," another boy yelled out.

"Well, if you're looking for a fight, here I am," Peter yelled as he through his book bag to the floor. He tried to control himself, but he couldn't.

"Boy, I'll beat you done like you stole something. You're just a dirty ass White boy who needs to be with their own kind."

"Get out of my face. I'm tired of you people always messing with me. You're just a bunch of no good niggas who don't have anything else to do but start trouble."

The boys looked dumbfounded. "Screw you," the leader of the group spoke as he pushed Peter down and they all walked off. They thought it would make him angrier, but he didn't care any way.

When Peter made it to his seat the teacher came in, "Settle down class and get out your homework. We have a few things to discuss."

A girl tapped Peter on the shoulder. When he turned around she was very bright skinned, long pig hair, green eyes, and beautiful. She spoke, "You want to be my boyfriend. We can kiss and stuff."

Peter had to admit she was beautiful, but he could see that she wasn't White. He felt angry because since he walked into the class Black people had been nothing but trouble for him. His mind was on his studies so he could make real money.

I don't have any time wasted on poor conversations with these people, he thought. Therefore, he turned to the little girl and spoke softly to her, "I don't know why your kind always tries to go with me. I don't want you all. Your skin is not light enough, your long hairs has naps, your ignorant, and if it was like mine we may be able to talk, until then stick to your own league."

She could only respond, "Peter Brennan you pumpkin eater, you'll never have a girl. You'll never keep her. You think you're smart, think you're all that but the girl you love she will be fat."

Peter stood up in front of the entire class and blurted out, Can you leave me alone. All you niggas in here can leave me alone. I'm so tired of you all trying to bully me. I'm tired of you all girls trying to like me. I hate Black people. Leave me the hell alone."

When he said that the class was quiet and everyone was shocked so the teacher made him get in the hall until the class left out.

"Peter, you can go stand in the hall until I finish."

"I don't care about standing in the hall. The walls like me better anyway," Peter replied as he jumped up and walked out the classroom slamming the door.

The teacher finished class and rushed outside to talk to Peter. She's never seen him in this state of mind.

"Peter Brennan, we do not put others beneath us and we don't talk about race. We are all the same on the inside and nurtured with love. You are Black just like the rest of us. I don't ever want to hear you use that "N" word again," his teacher said.

"You mean the word nigga?"

"What did I say? Don't say it ever again," she replied with a mean look.

"I don't care anymore. I'm tired of everyone picking on me and calling me a cracker. Do you know how that feels to have your own people hate you?"

"Peter, people don't hate you. They don't have a good understanding about those types of things. You can't think negative like everyone else. You have to be you. Why do you insist on stereotyping Black people? Your mother is Black," she asked.

"I stereotype because I wonder why do

more Blacks live in poverty and think low of themselves."

"People have many situations to come on them and how they handle them is up to their discretion," The teacher replied.

"I understand, but tell those people to leave me alone I don't want them, they are trouble and that is something I don't have time for," Peter said seriously.

"Peter, I will not warn you again. As for them staying away from you I will tell them to leave you alone. If this happens again of this name calling, I will call your mother and you will go to the office. Racist behavior will not be tolerated in my class and nowhere else on school grounds," The teacher said a little louder.

"Ma'am, as for my mother you can call her. She's Black and maybe she would understand better than me. I'm sure she would understand of how you people think," Peter remarked as he walked off. He looked back to see that dumb founded look on his teachers face.

Chapter 7

Abby arrived at the hospital on two wheels. She drove up to the emergency exit, people rushed to move back. She ran through the door as she carried Alex like a baby while Peter was beside her and he held onto her shirt tail. A nurse ran up and took Alex. By that time, he was unconscious.

"What happened?" a small figured nurse asked.

"We were working in the garden and a snake bit him in the face."

"Is the rest of you okay?"

"Yes, please help my son," Abby plead as she began to cry.

The nurse handed Alex to a young doctor and they rushed off to the back. Two men brought a stretcher and placed Alex on it. Abby put her head down as Peter looked into her face and wrapped his arms around her waist.

"I love you, mother," Peter said.

Abby didn't say a word, only rubbed his head. Peter continued to look into her face only to see hurt. He only wanted to comfort his mother, but her mind was on Alex.

The doctor rushed back in, "Ma'am, do you know what type of snake that bit your son?"

"Yes sir, it was a garden snake. Is he going to be alright?"

"We are going to do everything we possibly can to save him."

"Mother, he was all Black," Peter interrupted.

"Are you sure, I thought it was a garden snake."

"Yes, ma'am, I am sure. He was all Black."

"Good looking out, young man," the doctor stated and went to the back.

The doctor left and Abby put her arm around Peter. They walked to the small waiting area and sat down. Peter held his head low.

"Are you alright?" she asked.

"Do you blame me, mother?"

"No baby. Why would you say that?"

"Because Alex was protecting me. He always protects me and gets hurt."

"That's nonsense, Peter. We all were at the wrong place at the wrong time."

"I wonder mother, do you love me?"

Peter asked.

"Yes, you are my son. You are my flesh and blood. I will always love you."

"I love you, too."

"Why do you keep asking me that?"

"Because we have different fathers. Mine is White, and not Black."

"Boy, are you serious? That has nothing to do with me loving you or Alex. I don't care if your father is purple. It's true you and Alex have two different fathers and they are of two different races, but that doesn't matter. I treat both of you the same and I love you both the same. Don't ever, ever forget that I love you. Understand?"

"Yes, mother."

She grabbed Peter and squeezed him tightly, to assure him that she love him. He had always doubted his mother's love. Peter hugged Abby and smiled with happiness, but in the back of his mind he thought of his father every day. He remembers how he smelled, the curves on his round face with a mixture of blonde and brown hair. He held Abby closer sniffing and smelling her. Her scent smelled of fruits as with his father smelled muskier.

Abby looked outside through the window and wondered if Alex would be okay. Was Peter right? Was it his fault? It was true that Alex protected him all the time and got hurt. She wished that Peter would protect himself. He acted so fragile at times. But, it wasn't his fault he acted that way. She was the same way when she was smaller. Abby's thought went back to when she was in high school. Girls her age beat her up all the time. She got so scared one time thinking she was going to die. Three girl's grades above her were tossing her book bag around. She kicked the little fat chubby girl in the leg. The girl screamed out but jumped on Abby until she fell to the ground. The fat girl pounded Abby's head against the cement floor until a teacher broke it up. Her head was bleeding real badly. Her parents were called and she was rushed to the emergency room getting eight stitches to the back of her head. Her thoughts were interrupted as the doctor came in.

"Ms. Brenner, I have some good news."

"Yes sir."

"The both of you can go in and see him now."

"Is he going to be alright?"

"Yes ma'am. He's a little groggy, but

fine. He's a strong young man."

"Thank you, sir, for saving my baby," she stated as she gave him a friendly hug.

Abby grabbed Peter's hand as the doctor took them up to Alex's room. As they approached the room, Peter rushed up to the bed and looked at Alex. He had a bandage on his face, and his eyes popped open as soon at Peter jumped on the bed. Peter grabbed his hand and sat down while Abby walked to the other side of the bed. Alex looked at her and tears fell down his face. Abby cried because her child laid in the bed hurt. She was supposed to be there to protect him, but instead, he laid there hurt.

"Mama, don't cry. I am okay," Alex stated.

"I know, baby, but I am supposed to protect you."

"I'm a big boy. I will always protect you and Peter."

Peter looked at Abby as she stared at Alex. Her baby was in the hospital so he tried to be a man.

"I told you I would protect you," Alex told Peter while he looked into his eyes.

"I know. I'm sorry you got hurt."

Peter smiled at Alex and squeezed his hand. Alex slid over and Peter hopped into the bed with him. They both lay there while they stared into the ceiling as Abby took a seat. She put her head into her hands and thanked God that her son would be okay.

Abby jumped up from the chair and walked over to the hospital bed. "Take each other's hand we need to pray. The boys held each other's hand and bowed their heads. My Dear Father in heaven, Thank you for saving Alex life. He's been a strong young man over the years with protecting me and Peter. Lord, guide me in the right direction to help keep my family safe. I've done so much but it feels like it's not enough. Protect us in Jesus name. Amen."

Alex blurted out, "God please protect my mother and let her know that no matter what I will always be by her side. Amen. Alex looked up at Abby with that big bright Colgate smile. Peter smiled but directed his attention towards the window as big balls of rain drop attacked the window.

Chapter 8

Weeks passed by and it got more and more stressful for her trying to prove her love to Peter. It seemed like the older he got, the more he wanted to be loved. He desired his father in his life, but she didn't know where he was. Plus, she really didn't care to know after he beat her down like a dog. How could someone deny a child? Children were so fragile and innocent. She didn't understand why Joseph acted the way he did. How could he deny loving her? Her memory flashed back to when she overheard Joseph and his father, Thomas, talking about getting rid of her and her baby. The news of being a first time father had blown Joseph away. He loved Abby and admitted that it would be tough on them because of their race, but he loved her enough to do his best. But, what he didn't know is that his father had another thing in mind. It took him a long time to conquer his father and that could destroy them. Joseph started to work with his father after he got the job winning a scholarship after graduating from college. That was a dream come true for Joseph.

Joseph knew he must go on and tell his father before anyone else did. He knows that his father would not approve, but knew if he set his mind on something he would do it with or without his help. He believed it was his business and what he did should not affect the company; however, he walks slowly knowing the task would not be that easy. Abby stood back watching and when he entered his father's office, she stepped next to the door listening in on their conversation.

Joseph knocked on the door and enters. His father had waited on him all day. He knew his son was simple minded and would want to marry the Black woman. Thomas knew that something had to be done to break up that sham of a relationship.

"Come in son," his father yells out as he covers the mouth piece of the phone."

"I'll be with you in one moment."

Joseph looks up and hears his father say goodbye to the person on the other end of the phone. "I hope you have great news that inquires more money to be made? You know a man can never have enough money."

"Not quite. There's something you need to hear from me. In fact I know that you will not approve of this but," Joseph spoke but before he could finish his sentence his father replied, "You got that nigga pregnant?"

Joseph was quiet and didn't know what to expect, so his father repeated it again a little louder, but with an attitude, "You got that nigga pregnant, didn't you?"

With the warmest smile Joseph replied "Yes, Abby is pregnant. Dad you could learn to like her. She is really the sweetest person I have ever met. She really makes me happy. I never thought I would find love like this."

Joseph said with a dreamy look on his face. It is the kind of look that Thomas would wipe off his face and snap his son into reality. Joseph rose up and continued, "She knows me like the back of her hands and this joy I feel for her I just didn't think possible. I am happy dad and I intend to marry her."

Thomas believed that his son was easy, but he never thought about him trying to marry a nigga. *This must be stopped*, he thought. Thomas rose, places his elbows on the desk, folded his hands under in front of his mouth, and his thumbs under his chin, then replies, "I can't let you marry that girl.

Find you a White woman. Shit, I'll help you find one just don't disgrace our family by not marrying your own kind."

While he waited on a reply from his son he sat back into his chair and continues, "Surely she was just a rump in the hay? For heaven sakes boy, she is Black. You can find her type all day every day. Joseph, she is someone that is only a thrill and not important enough to settle down with. You have money and can buy as much ass as you desire. Son, you have your entire life a head of you. Why waste it on this coon?"

"Stop with the name calling. That's not going to make me change my mind. Father she means more to me than that. She is beautiful, has her head on right and she is carrying my first baby. Give her a chance."

His father shakes his head as he continues to sit back onto his huge leather chair and sighs loudly, "Get your head out of her ass. The girl is Black. There is nothing she can do for you besides satisfy you in bed. Leave that nigga where she is. Her kind will bring you down and destroy everything you have. Get for real boy, take your head out of your pants and put it on straight. Tell me what she plans to do about the baby? The baby you sure it's yours and not someone else's she is trying to pass off to obtain money from you. Her type of people will swindle you dry if you let them, my son," His father said in a voice that hoped she would abort it.

"I know it is my child she carries. That much I am sure of, dad. I can't say what Black people would do, but I know she is not like that and we plan to keep it and possible marry."

"Marry! Marry!" His father yelled loud as people outside the office stopped working to listen. "That is a little too much. I won't allow it. Do you hear me boy? Give her money and let her abort the damn thing. You have a lot riding on this and you don't need this junk clouding your judgment."

"Abort it? Father, never that! We are keeping it and I love her. I understand you are angry, but you need to realize that it is my life."

"If you choose to be with her then I have no choice, but to disown you as my son. I will not allow any of my seed to be with a Black woman. Niggas are made for the cotton fields, not lay in our beds and become wives."

"Father, you don't mean this," Joseph replied.

"Yes my son, this is your decision. You choose it is your family or some nigga you decided to sleep with and got pregnant," Thomas asked with a steer voice.

"I will never turn my back on my family," Joseph spoke as he rose from his chair and walked out. Abby stood frozen next to the wall. Joseph stepped out and saw her there crying. He looked at Abby and walked away. Abby stepped out into the door way to have a good look at Joseph. He turned around and gave her this dirty smile. Abby put her head down and walked out.

Abby sat down on her bed and stared at the wall. Her thoughts went back to when Peter asked her if she loved Alex more than she loved him. Her love was equal. *Where was he getting all those crazy ideas?* She wondered. She prayed that her father didn't have anything to do with it. He sometimes looked at Peter like he could kill him. That was why she didn't allow them to visit their grandparents without her. Her father already hated her. *He told her he hated her to her face. How could a father not love his child?* She thought. She would never act like toward her children. She would always protect and love them. She got down on her knees and began praying to God.

"My God, my one true Savior, I have struggled and struggled trying to love my kids. I don't understand why Peter thinks I love Alex more than I love him. I know that Peter blames me because he is mixed racially, but I couldn't help who I loved. I love both my children, unconditionally. There is nothing in this world that I would or wouldn't do for them. What am I doing wrong? Help me, Lord. I don't show favoritism between the two. I try to provide a safe home, but this old house is coming down. Help me to better myself so I can provide for my children the way I need to. I hate being on welfare, but that's how we ate. My kids look at me like they hate me sometimes. I rebuke that devil. Lord, please hold my family together as one. Help me, Lord. You say ask and I shall receive."

After the short prayer, Abby got ready for bed. She looked in the corner at a big crack on the floor. She could see the outside. In the morning, she tried to patch it up or stick some clothes in it. She knew that it wouldn't be long before the house crumbled down, but she had no other place to go. Suddenly, it began to rain. She could hear the rain hit against the tin roof. Abby jumped up to place buckets and bowls all over the house to keep the rain from destroying it. The living room was the worst. She had put a big, black garbage bag up to keep the rain out, but it still leaked because the roof had a big hole in it. Abby put the buckets down in the living room and walked out. She could hear Alex and Peter as they moved their bed around.

She walked in their room to help them move the bunk bed around, and saw there was a small leak right above the bed. Peter ran to get a bucket while Alex and Abby finished rearranging things. Peter placed the bucket on the floor under the leak, and all three of them stood there and stared at the bucket as the water drip faster and faster. Alex looked at Abby and jumped into the bed. His expression on his face proved that he was pissed. She already knew what was on his mind.

"Did you boys put buckets down for the rest of the house?"

"Yes, ma'am," Peter replied.

"Thank you, baby," Abby said as she put her arm around Peter.

"Mama, are you not tired of living in this dump," Alex blurted out putting a damper on the conversation.

"This is not a dump. This is our home.

The answer to your question is yes. I would love to live in a big brick house like your grandparents have. I just can't afford it right now."

"You always give that lame excuse. Come up with something better to tell us because we're heard that one many times."

"Don't you dare talk to me like that Alex Brenner," Abby spoke as she poked Alex in the chest. He slapped her hand down saying, "I see why Peter doesn't want to be here. We try to make you happy, but what about us. We want to be happy, too. It's not all about you, Abby," Alex barked. Abby raised her hand to slapped the taste out of his mouth, but put her hand down. She shoved him towards the bed, "Go to bed, Alex. We will finish this conversation tomorrow."

Alex looked at the two of them and jumped into bed. He wanted to move. He was tired of living in an old, run down house with holes all around. In some spots, you could see the ground. They were lucky a snake or lizard hadn't crawled in.

"Well, Peter, go to bed and get some rest."

"Okay, mother."

"Good night, Alex," Abby said.

He didn't respond. Sometimes, his attitude was bad, but she still loved him despite it.

Peter jumped into bed and said, "I love you, mother."

"I love you, too, baby." She kissed him on the jaw. She looked down at Alex. She wanted to kiss him goodnight, but she didn't want to go through all the drama. Sometimes, Alex gave her hell when he was pissed off. Peter could, too, but not like Alex. She remembered the first time she had to spank Alex.

"What seems to be your problem ,Alex? Peter?"

"I'm so tired of those boys picking on Peter. I'm going to go get grandfather's gun and shoot them," Alex threatened.

"Alex, are you crazy? I don't ever want to hear you threaten to harm another person. Is that understood?"

"No mama, it's not understood. You're not the one who has to protect him over and over. I have to fight almost every day. I'm going to show all of them not to mess with my brother," Alex harshly spoke.

"Alex, you don't have to fight for me no more. I can take care of myself," Peter interrupted.

"Sure you can. You can take care of yourself just like mama can take care of us."

"What's that supposed to mean, Alex? I'm working my butt off to provide for you two," Abby defended.

"Work hard for what mama? To give us old clothes from the Salvation Army or asking the welfare people to help feed up," Alex barked with so much attitude it pissed Abby off.

"Go get my belt Alex, now." Alex didn't move he just stared at his mother.

"Go get my belt, Peter. Alex thinks I'm playing with him."

"Please, mother, don't whip him. I promise to protect myself. Please don't whip him," Peter begged.

"You don't have to worry about me, Peter. I'm going to get that gun and shoot them all." Abby rushed to her bedroom and Alex stood in the middle of the room waiting on her to get back. Peter began to cry as Abby rushed back into the room with her long, black, leather belt. She began to whale on Alex with all the strength she had, but he never moved. He stood there like a man and waited for his mother to finish. "Are you finished?" Alex asked.

"Take your butt to bed and I don't

want to see your face no more tonight."

"Good, because I don't want to see yours either," Alex remarked as he grabbed the belt from Abby then throwing it out in the front yard.

"Go get that belt right now because I seriously beat you down," Abby threatened.

"You can go get it yourself. I'm tired of you, this house, Peter."

"Go to bed now."

"Can I eat first? Oh, my bad, mama. I guess I can go to bed hungry again," Alex replied as he stormed off to his bedroom. Abby was hurt that she has to whip Alex, but he was being too disrespectful. Then on top of that threaten to shoot people. That boy had a lot of nerve. Abby grabbed Peter who was sitting on the floor crying. She knew that something had to be done before she loses her sons.

Abby walked back to her room and sat down on the bed. She looked at the water that came into the house through the cracks and a tear fell down her face. She knew that something had to be done because it was pitiful. *How could I let my kids live like this?* She thought. She got into bed and cried herself to sleep like many other nights.

Alex and Peter lay silently in their

beds in their room. They lay on their sides, looked at the water drip into the bucket, and listened to their mother cry. Alex put his pillow over his ears so he didn't have to hear her cry.

"Did you know that you hurt her feelings tonight?" Peter told Alex as he rolled over looking into the ceiling.

"I don't care. I'm so tired of all this mess. Our life shouldn't be like this. Why is she making us suffering like this?" Alex asked.

"I don't know, but my dream is to go be with my father one day. My dream is to never live like poor people. I have big dreams and they will soon come true."

"What are you so called big dreams?"

"That's to become one of the world's richest people. I want to have enough money to eat whatever I want, live in a huge house with so many rooms, and have a big family," Peter replied.

"Well keep dreaming because this is your life, now. Living in a hut with hardly anything to eat. I hate this place."

"You'll see one day Alex. I will show the world that I'm a good person and I deserve better than this," Peter spoke as he stared at the ceiling thinking about his future.

Chapter 9

A couple of days had done by and everything seemed great until the day Abby's mother rushed to let her know what had happened.

"Abby, it's your mother open the door," Rose yelled as she banged loudly.

"What's wrong?" Abby yelled as she rushed to open the door.

"It's the boys. We received a call from Chief Booker saying he had the boys down at the station."

"That can't be possible. Their sleep," Abby replied as she rushed to their room and the beds were empty.

"What did they do? Oh my God, did Alex get daddy's gun."

"Goodness no, Abby why would he do that."

"It's a long story mama. What's wrong?"

"They stole your father's truck and wrecked it. They called the house to let us know they that are safe at the station," Rose replied as Abby put on her clothes.

"Does daddy know?"

"I'm afraid he does. He's at the house ramping and raving. Abby your father is very upset. Make sure you hurry up and get down there before he does."

"I'm headed out now. What on earth would make them steal daddy's truck?"

"Go and find out Abby. Make sure they are safe."

"I'm going mama. I'll let you know everything as soon as I find out what's going on with them," Abby replied as she grabbed her keys and rushed off.

Abby pulled up at the police station very worried. She couldn't believe they had stolen her father's truck. Abby rushed into the station, ready to kill them because they knew better.

"Hi, Abby," Chief Booker said as he took off his hat.

"Hey, where are Alex and Peter?"

"I have them in a cell."

"What happened?" she asked in shock.

"Well, I was driving home and I saw your father's truck moving very slow down the street. I waved and Alex ducked down, so I pulled the truck over. He kept going. I had to get another deputy to pull in front of them. We stopped the truck and I placed them in the car. I didn't impound your father's truck, but I called him. He's on his way down."

Abby sighed. "Oh my God, are you serious? All I need is my father here."

Abby and Chief Booker walked to the back to the jail cells. Peter and Alex jumped up as soon as they saw their mother. Chief Booker unlocked the cell doors and before Abby could say anything, she heard her father's voice.

"I'm going to whip them boys' asses. They better not have messed up my truck."

Chief Booker grabbed John because he tried to go in the cell. Abby stood at the door to block him from entering.

"Abby, I'm going to whip their asses. They know better."

"Dad, I will handle this."

"I've sat back long enough watching you and your brats. Your mama has always saved you, but not this time."

"John get out of here. You need to calm down," Chief Booker stated.

"I'm calm. I'm whipping those boys' ass."

"Not my sons," Abby spoke.

"That's the problem. You running around here like they are innocent. I know that half breed talked Alex into stealing my truck."

"Don't you dare call my son a half breed. He's Black just like Alex. I'm tired of you trying to separate my kids."

"Well, I hate that boy and you. You are not my child. The worst mistake I could have made was having you."

"I don't care how you take to me, but you will not talk about my son like that."

"Your mother should have aborted you, too. I don't know what I was thinking in the first place. You and your kids are a bunch of headaches. Don't ever be caught back around my house again," John threatened.

Abby stood there looking at her father say all those things. She was very hurt, but she stood her ground. Chief Booker pushed John out of the room. Abby stood there while she stared at Peter and Alex, who stood there looking at her. They heard every word. She wished that they didn't have to witness that.

"Come on, boys, let's go."

"Mother, we are so sorry for taking the truck. We were headed to the store to buy some snacks," Peter said.

"It was my idea," Alex stated.

"It doesn't matter, you boys knew better. Why you didn't just take my car? You just had to take your grandfather's truck?" she said as she sighed.

"We are so sorry, mama," Peter apologized.

"Yes, mother, we are sorry. I took the truck and I apologize."

Abby, Peter, and Alex walked up to the front. She hoped that her father was gone, but her wish didn't come true.

"I want to press charges," he yelled out while looking at Peter and Alex.

"John, be sure this is what you want. These are your grandchildren," Chief Booker said.

"You two boys have lost your minds taking my truck. You should have taken your mother's beat up ass car."

"Well, John, we can write out the papers if you are serious."

"They need to be taught a lesson since their mother has no idea how to raise children."

John looked over at the boys and threw his hat down on the ground. He kicked the hat into the air. Peter and Alex looked as if they were lost.

"Forget it, Tim. If Alex wasn't

involved I would have, but I'm not going to."

"Okay, John."

"How in the hell did you boys start my truck?" John asked.

"I knew where you kept your spare key," Alex stated.

"Alex, goddamn it. I can't believe you. Did that boy talk you into stealing my truck?"

"No, grandpa, I did it all by myself."

"Well, I just don't believe that shit."

Chief Booker and Abby looked at each other. John gave Peter a weird look, and if looks could kill, Peter would have been dead.

"Chief Booker, are the boys free to go?" Abby asked as she looked at her father.

"Yes, Abby. They are lucky that I know you. If they were in another city, they would be headed to jail for auto theft."

"Yes, I know. Thank you, Chief Booker, for calling us. It won't happen again."

"You right, not with my truck," John added.

"Dad, you have your truck. Now go home."

"If you raised them right, then all this

wouldn't have happened."

"I did raise my son's right."

"Sure you did. That half breed is the oldest. He should have known better."

"Stop calling my son a half breed. You are really about to piss me off."

"Don't you talk to me like that girl?"

"Well, stop trying to discriminate against my child. He is my son and if you don't like it then you can go to hell." John rushed up to Abby and slapped her across the face sending her body to the ground. Alex and Peter rushed to her side.

"Don't you ever hit my mama again," Peter yelled.

"You son of a…." John spoke as he held up his hand to strike Peter, but Chief Booker caught his hand.

"John, I think it's time for you to go. Too much has been said already. You need to go home and cool down," Chief Booker spoke.

John looked at Abby and walked out. He wanted to curse her out and beat her down, but he didn't. He didn't for two reasons. One was because she was his daughter, and two, Rose, his wife would kill him.

Abby, Peter, and Alex walked out a

few minutes after John. Chief Booker looked at Abby and stated, "He's set in his ways. Overlook him."

"I know, Chief Booker, thank you."

"Your father has spoken some horrible things. Just keep your head up and don't let him separate your family."

"I don't understand why he hates Peter so much."

"Because John knows that Peter's father is White. Back in his days, Black was treated like nothing. We were beaten, our Black women were raped, and he can't get past that. He probably feels like you betrayed your family. I know I would," Chief Booker spoke as he looked at Abby.

Abby looked at him and they exited the door. Chief Booker looked out the door at them as they left the station and shook his head. He couldn't believe that John acted that way toward his daughter. He wished he still had his daughter, but she died. She was killed by a drunk driver. He would give the world to love and touch his daughter again.

After that night, things looked a little bit better. Peter and Alex apologized every day to Abby about stealing the truck. They were so lucky that Abby forgave them, but their grandfather didn't forget. He didn't talk to the boys for a while. Abby didn't care because he always tried to separate them. She wished he would stop that mess. It was her family, not strangers, and his family, too. *What was the problem with him? Being a racist, old fool was his problem*, she thought.

She prayed that things would get better. Things had to get better.

Chapter 10

Abby and her boys walked down the dirt road carrying jugs of water. The water in the house wasn't drinkable because the pipes were old and rusty, but she hoped to get them fixed one day. Plus, her brother Mike ran off with her car and hadn't returned. Until then, they would continue to carry water from her parents' house. As they walked, she looked back at her sons, and knew they were tired of doing that. She prayed that God would find a way to make things better.

"When I grow up, I will never live like this," Peter spoke.

"Me either. I will live in the biggest house and drive a nice ride," Alex replied.

"I hate living poor," Peter said as he held his head down.

"We can run away," Alex suggested.

"And, go where?"

"I don't know, but we can figure something out."

"If we leave, then what about mother?"

"You're right. I don't want to leave her

behind, but we can come back to get her one day. I hate for her to be alone though," Alex replied.

"She won't be alone. She has our grandparents. We have to better ourselves."

'Remember grandfather told her not to come back to his house again. We can't leave her alone."

Alex looked over at Peter with unhappiness. They carried the water in the house and placed it on the floor next to the small deep freezer. Alex and Peter looked at each other, and then Peter fiddled with his left ear. He always did that when he was nervous or scared about something.

"What is it? Why you two staring at me?" Abby asked.

"Mother, why are we living so poor? You can do better. I know this," Alex blurted out.

"It's not by choice. We have no other place to go. How many times are we going to go over this conversation?"

"I don't believe that," Peter said.

"There are other houses or apartments, we can get or move in with grandma and grandpa," Alex spoke with a little bass in his voice.

"No," Peter yelled out.

"Why not?" Alex asked.

"I don't feel comfortable at their house. Grandpa John hates me."

"He doesn't hate you," Abby said.

"Yes, he does. You look at me like he does some times."

"Don't start this, Peter. I will never hate you."

"Well, I'm moving in with them and you can't stop me," Alex told them.

"Don't talk crazy."

"I'm serious," Alex said.

"Well, I'm tired of you having us live like a slave," Peter barked.

"Peter, how dare you," she spoke.

"He is right, you got us living off welfare, living in a shack, and you don't give a fuck!" Alex yelled out.

"Alex!" Abby yelled as she slapped him across the face.

Peter jumped because the slap was very loud. She tried to slap the taste out of Alex's mouth for being disrespectful. Peter continued to fiddle with his ear and stared at Alex. Alex pushed Abby and ran out the door then Peter ran after him. Abby stood at the back door as she watched her sons run down the dirt road toward her parents' house. After they disappeared out of sight, she sat down and stared out into the woods. Alex and Peter were right. They lived like slaves. That old house her parents passed down was so unfit to stay in, but it was the best she could do. She worked part-time, but that wasn't enough money.

Tears fell down her face. She didn't know what else she could do. It had gotten so bad that her children turned against her. Abby pray every day that the Lord would keep them together as one.

She had to do better because it was about to tear her family apart. She looked up toward the sky and said, "Lord, please help me. I'm losing my children." Abby got down on her knees and cried. Her only thoughts were of Joseph. "Damn you Joseph. You promised to take care of me and my kids. You lied to me. You lied to me."

Chapter 11

"Alex!" Peter yelled out while he ran down the dirt road.

Alex looked back and stopped. They looked at each other, and then walked together with their heads down. Peter touched Alex on the face where Abby slapped him, but Alex moved away with attitude.

"What are we going to do to help mother?" Peter asked.

"I don't know. I can't believe mama slapped me."

"Me either, but I think we hurt her feelings."

"Yeah, we did, but I hate living poor. We aren't slaves. I want new clothes, new shoes, but instead, I get hand me downs from God knows who," Alex expressed.

"Look at these shoes. These buddies," Peter joked.

They laughed and play fight, and then they raced each other down the road. After all the horseplay, they walked quietly, and wondered what in the world would they do to help their mother.

"What's the plan?" Peter fiddled with his ear.

"I don't want to go back to that house."

"Let's go to Grandma's house and stay. She won't turn us down."

"You right, she has a four bedroom brick house. She and Grandpa John are the only ones living there."

"I wonder why mama doesn't want to live with them."

"Who knows? Probably because Grandpa John doesn't like her," Alex spoke.

"In a way, I don't want to live with them. You know he told mother not to ever come back over there." Peter whined.

"Why not? He told her not us."

"He hates me and I feel so bad when I'm around him."

"You right Peter. I will protect you if anything happens. I just don't want to go back to that hut anymore."

"He hates her like he does me. Suppose you're not around when he does try to hurt me Alex."

"I will always be around to protect you even when you're not looking. I don't' understand how a person can hate their own child?" Alex said while picking up a rock and throwing it into the woods.

They continued to walk down the road in silence until they got to their grandparents' house. As they arrived, they saw Grandma Rose sitting on the porch. They had to tell her what happened.

Chapter 12

When they walked up, Grandma Rose was sitting on the porch shelling a bucket of purple hull peas that she got from the garden.

"What are you boys doing over there?"

They ran up to her and kissed her on each cheek at the same time.

"Well, Grandma Rose, we had a fight with mama."

"A fight?"

"I mean an argument. We don't want to live poor anymore. I hate it," Alex stated.

"Me, too, Grandma," Peter said.

"We have rags for clothes, our shoes are so old that you can see the bottom of my feet, and our house is so run down and old," Alex added.

"I understand, baby, that you two don't want to live poor. I say help your mother out. You boys are big enough to work."

"We want to work, but where?"

"Don't know, but you have to realize that you boys are teenagers and are soon to be men. Your mother is struggling. We tried to help, but Abby is so stubborn and refuses help from us."

"But, why?" Peter asked.

"Abby is like her father, too much pride to ask for help."

"Well, I'm not going back. I'll run away from home rather than go back to that shack, Alex spoke."

"Don't leave me out. I'm running away, too," Peter added.

"If you abandon your mother, who will protect her? She loves you boys so much. And, Peter, she had you at fifteen and Alex at seventeen years old. She was a young mother, but continued to support and raise you two," Grandma Rose explained.

They all stared into the woods. There was silence for a few minutes, but Grandma Rose continued on.

"I shall not lie, your grandfather tried to give you two away to a better family, but Abby moved out at seventeen and stood her ground. She quit school and worked at the Highly Grocery Store to support you two. Your mother is a strong woman."

"That's sounds good, but she needs to get out of that house," Alex said.

"Well, I would like to know where my

father. Is he still alive?"

Rose sighed at the thought of answering that question. She knew that Abby hadn't told them anything about their fathers. She feared they would run away to try to find their fathers. She didn't want to lose her children to men that didn't want them.

"Peter, your father left your mother before she delivered you."

"What happened? Every time I ask her about him, she just goes in her room and closes the door."

"Well, Abby and your father were very much in love with each other. They met at the Highly Grocery Store. Your grandpa tried to keep them apart because he knew there was still racism in this world. There are a lot of White people that hate Black people and a lot Black people who hate White people. But, it didn't matter, those two were not separating. Joseph came down here every day to see Abby. We kept running him off. Then, one day Abby tells us she pregnant. We tried to get her an abortion, but she was too far gone."

"Why did you try to get rid of me?" Peter asked with disappointment in his face.

"Don't be sad, Peter, you are here

now. That's the good thing. Anyway, your grandfather marched Abby over to Joseph's parents' house and showed his tail."

Peter asked, "What did Grandpa John say?"

"I can't go into details, but it wasn't good. We found out later that Joseph's father beat him up bad. Your grandfather beat Abby, but I stopped him. A week later, Joseph came down here. He tricked Abby outside and beat her like a dog. He said she was a dumb nigga to get pregnant. Abby was hospitalized."

Peter looked at Alex as he held his head down with a disappointed look. Peter stared at Grandma Rose, and then spoke, "But, why he didn't want me either?"

"No, he didn't because his folks hated Black people. But, Joseph loved him some Abby. Abby told me that they talked and he wanted her to kill the baby. She told him no, that it was too late, but he became very angry and beat Abby near death. The good thing is he tried to kill you while you were still inside your mother, but he didn't. Abby was very strong and she held him off from kicking her in the stomach. After that, we never saw Joseph again."

"Did he go to jail?" Peter asked.

"Heavens no, Abby lied and said some strange Black man jumped her, but later she told me the truth. I never told anyone else besides your Grandpa John. By then, he was ready to kill Joseph's whole family."

Peter leaped up off the porch. "If I ever lay eyes on him, I will kill him for hurting my mother."

"Yeah, if you ever find him."

"Man, forget him," Alex said as he wrapped his arm around Peter.

"Yeah, but he didn't have to do her like that."

"Well, my father probably did the same thing."

"No, Alex, it was totally different. Abby was being wild and got pregnant. We did blood tests with two boys and got the right one. But, he didn't want Abby or you. He had just married another girl from across the way."

"It doesn't matter. I will show my mother much love."

"Both of you boys need to shower your mother with love because she had been through so much to keep you all as a family," Rose told them.

"Alex, I'm going home to my mother," Peter stated.

"Let's go and apologize. I feel so bad about what I said to mama," Alex said.

They kissed Grandma Rose on her cheeks and left running back home to apologize to their mother. Rose looked as they ran down the street.
Suddenly, Grandpa John stepped out the door. He watched them run like rabbits down the road.

"Why you tell them the truth?" he asked Rose.

"Because they deserve the truth, how Abby suffered to keep them. She has been through a lot."

"She was stupid and young. She should have let me get rid of those boys when I had the chance," John said as he walked back into the house.

Rose looked at John with an evil look on her face, and then she yelled, "Well, it's love for her children. Maybe you need to show love to your own kids."

Rose got her cane, stepped off the porch, and walked over to her garden. She talked to herself because John really pissed her off. She thought that he needed to show Abby some love. He loved all thirteen of his kids, but couldn't stand Abby. It was true she went against his will to love a White man, but it was over. He hated Abby for disobeying him. He should love his child no matter what she had done. Why couldn't John just forgive and forget?

Chapter 13

Alex and Peter ran all the way back home. It was dark and about to storm again. As they approached the house, there were no lights on or any movement. They stopped and looked at each other. Then, they panicked and ran wildly toward the house. Alex jumped on the old porch and rushed through the front door. He turned on lights and called for his mom. Peter ran to Abby's bedroom and she wasn't there. He fiddled with his ear while looking at Alex. They both stood there looking at her bed.

"She is gone. She left us," Alex whispered.

"Heck no! I don't believe that. Mama wouldn't do that to us."

They looked around the house and found no Abby. Peter looked out the small, back kitchen window and saw his mother on her knees on the ground in the praying position. She looked up at the sky and called out to God.

"Alex, here's mama."

"Where?"

They both walked out the rusty

colored door and headed to the back of the house to pray with their mother. Whenever she was worried, that was what she always did. They approached Abby and kneeled down beside her. Abby began to recite Psalm 23. Alex and Peter recited it with her.

After praying, Abby stated, "Lord, please help me. Please, help me."

Tears fell down her cheeks as it began to rain. Alex and Peter began to cry with their mother because neither one of them wanted to see her suffer. It started raining harder.

Alex and Peter helped their mother off the ground, and after she stood up, she said, "I love you boys so much, and I promise that things will get better. I promise that our lives will change, starting tonight."

"Mama, it will be okay. Alex and I decided to get jobs to help out."

"Thank you, baby, but your mother will handle everything. I promise."

It began to thunder and lightning. Rain poured down while the trees swayed back and forth. They rushed in the house and closed the door. The wind blew so hard that the back door fell in. It was on one hinge and they had a table in the back of it to hold it up. The small kitchen window exploded, shards of glass hit Peter in the face. Abby rushed both the boys down the hall to the small bathroom and told them to stay there. They got in the tub and Peter began to panic. His face was bleeding from the glass and Alex took off his shirt and put it on Peter's face. Peter laid his head on Alex's shoulder.

Suddenly, the door swung open. Abby grabbed the boys and ran outside to her car. By that time, her father was driving up the driveway. They all jumped in the truck and took off. They headed to Abby parents' house.

After the rain calmed down, Rose looked out the window and saw smoke. She had a weird look on her face.

"What's wrong with you, mama?" Abby asked.

"I see smoke coming from over there by your place."

Abby rushed outside on the porch with the boys. They looked into the sky and it was filled with smoke. John and Rose came outside to join them.

"Mama, is that our house?" Peter asked.

"I don't know."

Grandpa John said, "Looks like it from here."

Abby began to panic. The rain had picked up a little more, but she didn't care. She jumped off the porch and began to run down the muddy road. Alex and Peter ran after her.

"Abby, come back!" Rose yelled.

"Let her go," John said.

"Shut up, John, you should have some compassion when it comes to your children."

"I do, just not toward her."

She stared at John for a few seconds. She saw why Abby was so protective of her children. Rose walked back into the house and slammed the door while John stood outside looking at the smoke.

Chapter 14

Abby, Peter, and Alex ran all the way to the house. As Abby got closer, she could see that her house was on fire and it was too late to save it. They stopped running and just stared. Abby began to cry while walking around in a circle holding her head.

"Mama, it will be alright. We are going to take care of you," Peter spoke.

"Yes, mama, it will be okay," Alex added.

Abby fell to the ground and cried. She got on her knees and asked God, "Why me? Why me?" She bent over putting her hands on the ground. She heard the siren of fire trucks rushing to get there, but it was too late. The house was gone. Two fire trucks showed up with three police cars and one ambulance. They stood by while the house continued to burn down.

By that time, Abby stood there holding her boys in each arm. Tears still flowed down her face, and Alex and Peter were sad, but happy at the same time.

Abby couldn't believe that she lost

everything. House, clothes, furniture, and even the car burned up. She put her head down. *Where will I live? How will I support my children?* All those thoughts crossed her mind. And, then, her parents drove up and got out. Rose put Alex and Peter in the truck while she and John stood out with Abby.

"What are you going to do?" Rose asked.

"I don't know. I guess we have to live in a shelter until I do better."

"Nonsense, you can live with us until you get on your feet."

"Mama, I don't want any charity," Abby stated.

"How is it charity? We are your parents. We are here to help," Rose offered.

"Well, she has to find a place to go. I don't want her or that White child living in my house," John said angrily.

"John, this is our child. And, I say she can live with us."

"She's your child, not mine. All my kids obey me."

"Mama, that's okay. We will find a shelter," Abby said softly.

"No, you won't. That's my house and I say you can stay," Rose said. She stared at John, wanting him to say something else.

She was going to throw his old ass out. There was no way she would turn her back on her daughter.

John walked off. He got back into the truck and stared at Rose. She knew that he was pissed, but she didn't care. Abby was her daughter, not some stranger.

"I can't believe that daddy still hasn't forgiven me."

"Abby, he's old. You are my child and I love you. You and your kids have a place to stay."

"Thank you, mama, but I need to do something fast."

"Forget about your father. I'm the boss. You and the boys will stay with us until you get on your feet. You are strong, Abby. Just pray about things and move on."

"I know, mama. I know," Abby said as she placed her arms around her mother.

Abby and her boys moved in with her parents. She knew that she would have to do something with the way her father walked around with hate in his eyes. He didn't want to have anything to do with either of them, but Alex had his heart. He would give Alex anything in the world he wanted. Abby hated the fact that he separated her children like that. It didn't matter if they were White or Black, they all were a family.

Abby went to work knowing she had to something that she never possibly thought she would do. The owner of the store was Mr. Tommy Hightower and he gave Abby the job. His son-in-law, Bill Tulane, ran the store and he was the one to hire and fire people. Bill had a thing for Abby, and he asked her for sex every day, offering her all kinds of money. She didn't want to say anything to anyone because that was the only job she had. She hated being at her parents' house. Her father's hate motivated her to swallow her pride. Something had to be done.

"Hi, Abby, I heard about what happened to your house. Let me know if you need anything," Bill said.

"Yes, sir," Abby said. She wanted to ask him if the offer still stood, about sex for money, but she couldn't bring herself to do it. He had a few warts here and there with red hair and freckles all over his face. His hair looked like *Fonzy* from *Happy Days*.

A week went by and finally, she gained up the nerves to approach him. Abby did notice that since her house burned down he never asked her for sex. She knew he wanted her to beg. She wasn't going to beg, she would ask one time and that was it. If he said no, then she wouldn't do it again. Before she could ask, he approached her.

"Hi Abby. How are you?" Bill asked.

"I am wonderful."

"Have you found you a place to stay?"

"Not yet, sir, I'm still living with my parents until I find something."

"Well, you know my wife owns those apartments across the bridge.

"Yes, sir, I know, but they are too expensive for me. Not with one job."

"Well, you know what you have to do to get what you want."

"What's that?"

"All I ask is once or twice a month and I will take care of you."

"You mean, to sleep with me you would provide a home for me and my kids?"

"Yes, a home and plenty of money to help out with your kids."

"Can you give me by the end of the day to think about it?"

"Yes, I will give you whatever you want."

Bill walked off and Abby stood there

thinking. He could be tricking her and then again, Bill was always a man of his word. Damn, she didn't want to screw for money, but she had no choice. Abby thought about the comments her kids had made. The look her father gave her and her son when they come around. She knew that Peter felt uncomfortable around him. She couldn't let him go through that. Forget it. Her mind was made up. She would go through with it.

Work was over with and Abby met with Bill at the Comfort Inn hotel in room 1026. The door was opened, so she walked in. Bill lay in the bed and she saw that he was already naked because his clothes were on the small couch.

"Hi, Abby, I'm so glad you decided to be with me."

Abby gave a fake smile. Bill jumped out of the bed and locked the door. His cock was very hard and standing out, and she figured him to be about seven inches. Abby was very nervous. She stood there while Bill fondled her clothes. He unbuttoned her shirt and threw it to the floor, and then lifted her bra over her breasts. He squeezed gently, and then he kissed them. He stopped and fully undressed her. She stood naked in front of her boss and it felt odd to her, but she had to do it.

After it was over with, Bill talked to Abby. "I know you didn't want to do it, but you had to do what you had to do. And, I promise that I won't go back on my word. How about I get a room with two queen size beds for you and your kids for about a week? That's how long it's going to take for me to get the apartment ready."

"What apartment?"

"I got an apartment for you and your kids. The paperwork will be ready in the next two days. I need you to sign a few things."

"Are you serious?"

"Yes, you will have a place to call home instead of living with your parents."

"Oh my God! Thank you so much for helping me."

"I know you didn't want to ask because you are stubborn at times. I'm the same way, but you deserve help."

"How can I afford it?"

"Leave it to me. This is one of our display apartments. We never use it. I told my wife about you and your children needing a home. She is willing to let you all live there for as long as you need to."

"This is so odd for me."

"I know, but I promised that I would take care of you. Just remember, I need you to take care of me, too, from time to time."

Bill got off the bed and gathered his pants. After he got dressed, he gave Abby a key.

"Here is the key to the other hotel room for you."

"Oh, you already got it?"

"Yes, I did. It's minutes from your job and the kids are in walking distance from school. I will try to rush the apartment. I will let you know tomorrow."

Bill looked at Abby and exited the door. Abby sat there on the bed looking at the hotel key. She got dressed and gathered her things, then headed to the other hotel room. It was room 1210, the last floor at the top. Abby opened the door and walked inside. There were two big beds, a flat screen TV on the wall, and a big bathroom. She walked over to the window and there was a big view of the city. It was getting dark and the light shined very bright. It lit the city of like a Christmas tree.

A Family Divided by Color

Abby was about to walk out when she saw an envelope laid out on the wooden table. She picked it up. It read: *Abby open me.*

She opened the letter and it had a lot of cash in it. Abby sat down on the bed holding the money. She counted every bit of it and it was $5,000 cash. She threw the money on the bed and fell down to her knees and prayed.

"Lord, please forgive me of my sins. I was wrong for sleeping with a married man, but I did it for my family. Lord, please forgive me of my sins."

Chapter 15

Things got better for Abby and her boys. Peter was finally off to college at Indiana State University while Alex attended Atlanta State University. Abby worked her ass off to get them there. She went back to school and got her high school diploma, then found a job at a software company. Abby got off welfare and bought a house, thanks to Bill Tulane. He had some pull and helped her. After the house, they called it quits. Abby was on her feet and headed in a new direction. She upgraded her vehicle to a 2005 Chevy Impala.

Alex and Peter had been gone for about a two years to college. The University of Atlanta was hosting a program for the gifted students and she would finally get a chance to see her boys again.

Every rock she made in her favorite chair she thought about Peter and how he ripped her heart. She knew she must be strong because her son was sought out from the beginning to understand the unexplainable. He always had an answer and for the most he was right on the money. *He hadn't written or even said thank you for loving him so much,* she thought, but her main thought was, *oh how I miss them both.* Even though, she talked to Alex on a regular basis, but Peter he was gone. Since graduation night he kept going and did not look back. In his mind, he was already gone he only was a visitor in her home. *He never seemed to fit in,* she thought. As Abby freshened up, Alex called.

"Hello."

"Hi, mama, how are you?"

"I'm wonderful now that I hear your voice. Have you heard from Peter?"

"No, I haven't talked to him in about a year. Have you?"

"No, I haven't talked to him since he went away to college. That's unusual for Peter to not call me."

"Yeah you're right. He's always been a mama's baby."

"Stop it," Abby joked.

"Yeah, yeah."

"I pray he is okay."

"Me, too. I've always had to protect him."

"It's okay, baby. Well, you get ready for this contest today."

"I'm ready, just waiting on you to get here."

"Okay, baby, I'm on my way."

After Abby hung up with Alex, she and David headed out. David and Abby had been together for about six months and madly in love with each other. Since the boys went away, David had been an Angel sent by God to her and after Peter left the way he did she may have been in shambles if David hadn't come along when he did. She had the complete empty nest feeling and it was hard to endure, but somehow David gave life a new meaning. *Marrying him was the best decision I made,* she thought as she saw him rowing up the garden. Since the boys went away, David was very protective of Abby because she was his heart.

They arrive at the university and the contest was held in the big stadium they recently built with the displays were on the floor. Everyone had to sit in the stands beside the immediate family and the judges. There were ten projects left, and only three would win. The 1st place winner would receive a trophy, $50,000 dollars, and a contract of any company they chose in their field. The 2nd place winner received a trophy and $25,000 dollars. The 3rd place winner received a trophy and $10,000 dollars. All of them were winners because it didn't look like a losing situation.

The judges checked each project. Peter built new software for computers to protect virus threats called BMAC Anti-Virus. And, Alex created a new kind of breathing machine to help people with asthma. The two boys were very creative and smart. Abby didn't realize how smart they were until that day.

On the first round, four people were eliminated, the second round, three people were eliminated, and it was down to the final round. It was Peter, Alex, and an Asian kid from Peter's school. His name was Pierre DuPont. He created a machine dealing with electric forensic fingerprinting. Abby thought all the project were excellent.

They announced Peter Joseph as the Grand Prize winner and he spoke, "I want to thank my family for being there supporting me through everything. They have showed me more love than I could have ever thought possible. If it hadn't been for you being there I would not be where I am now. Again, thank you dad for being there for me and loving me so much."

People clapped and Abby was stunned. They were in shock because he didn't mention them. Alex wasn't that surprised, but his mother was thrown for a loop. She never thought she would hear of him thanking the very people that destroyed her life and made her life with him hell. Abby just couldn't believe how flipped the script had become. She had to make her way to tell her how she felt about his so called thanking speech to his family.

Peter got first place, Pierre was second, and Alex was in third place. It didn't matter to Abby because her boys were perfect without a contest. After they announced the winners, the families were allowed to go down and greet the winners. Abby made it to the projects and Alex stood tall, so she went over to greet him first. Peter saw his mother go to Alex and he ran out of the building. Abby didn't see him leave as Alex greeted his mother with a big hug.

"Where's Peter?" Alex asked out with happiness.

"I don't know. He was standing over there by his project."

"I will go look for him," Alex said to his mother.

"Okay, baby, hurry up and come back. Other people want to greet you."

Abby and David walked over to Peter's project. They looked around, hoping to see Peter. A man and woman walk up to people, meeting and greeting them as if they were Peter's parents. The small woman announced, "We are sorry, everyone, but Peter has taken ill and had to leave. We are very sorry."

Abby walked up to her and asked, "He's sick, where is he?"

"Yes, ma'am, he is sick. Does Mr. Brenner know you?"

"Of course he does, I'm his mother, Abby Brenner."

"His mother?"

"Yes, his mother."

The lady put her hand to her chest, "Please, forgive me, ma'am. I wasn't trying to be rude. It's just that Peter told us that his mother was dead."

"What?"

The man and woman looked at each other and walked away as Abby began to get angry. Abby looked at David and he embraced her. While Alex ran off to find the unappreciated little brat of a brother of his. The man and woman looked at each other and walked away as Abby was angry.

"David," Abby said as if she was losing her breath.

"I can't breathe, help me," Abby said as she grabbed her chest and started hyperventilating.

While David helped Abby to the car, Alex searched for Peter and finally spotted him.

"Peter over here," Alex shouted with a loud angry voice.

Police stood nearby and Peter was surrounded by White boys that seemed to be educated. He stopped and looked at Alex, but he didn't speak. He tried to ignore his brother ,but Alex did not think that was the case, so he walked closer and said, "Peter, momma has been looking all over for you. Where you get off too? Why you dismiss us like that? "One boy asked, "Do you know that boy?"

Peter looked away from Alex and said, "No, that coon has me mixed up with somebody else."

They all laughed. Alex stood there with disappointment in his face because he heard what Peter said. *How could he deny him*? He thought Alex looked away, hoping his mother wasn't around to hear that mess. He took one last look at Peter, and another boy with Peter turned around and gave Alex the finger and walked off. Alex was about to go whoop his ass, but David grabbed his shoulders.

"Let's go. We have to comfort your mother right now."

"Why, what's wrong with her?"

"We just found out that Peter has told everyone that his mother is dead. There was a small, blond head woman walking around acting like his mother."

Alex turned around and looked at David. "He said his mother is dead?"

"Yes, that's what he says."

"Where's mama? Did she hear it?"

"Yes, I had to take her to the car. She is very hurt and she needs us."

They hurried back to the car. Alex opened the passenger door and held his mother. Tears fell down her face and it pissed Alex off.

"I love you, mama, please don't cry."

"What's wrong with Peter? Why does he say I'm dead?"

"I don't know. Don't worry about that clown."

Abby continued to cry. Alex gave her another big hug and kiss on the cheek.

"I'm going to find Peter and bust his head wide open."

"No. No. I don't want you two fighting. If that's what he wants, then let him be."

Alex jumped back from his mother and walked off to find Peter. Dave ran from around the car. He walked behind Alex and said, "What you going to do?"

"I'm going to kick his ass. This is our mother. Not some stranger."

He grabbed Alex arm and swung him around. "Just let him be. You can't make him want to love his mother. He has to want to do it himself. I don't know what his problem is. I don't know much about him, but I thought he was a good man."

"This is my brother. My flesh and blood. My best friend."

"I know it hurts, but he will come around."

Alex looked over at one of the buildings where he saw Peter and walked back to the car. He was hurt. Alex and David got in the car and they drove off. As they left the school property, Abby looked over and saw Peter being embraced by his father. Her face dropped. "What the..."

Peter looked at the car that drove by and immediately let go of his father. He and his mother's eyes locked.

"Pull over, David, pull over."

"No, Abby let him be."

Abby turned around fast and grabbed the steering wheel. David locked down on brakes. "Are you crazy Abby?"

Abby jumped out of the car and yelled out to Peter, "Are you serious? Are you fucking serious?"

"Come on, son," Joseph said as he spotted Abby and pushed Peter in a black, Cadillac Escalade truck.

Alex and David jumped out of the car as Joseph jumped in the truck and they drove off very fast. Abby stood there looking, and then she picked up a rock and threw it at the truck. "I can't believe this."

"Come on, Abby. Let's go home."

"Joseph has stolen my baby away from me. Oh my God. He's taken Peter away," Abby cried out as David embraced her.

Alex looked at her with hurt in his

face.

"Mama, you still got me."

Abby let go of David and embraced Alex. "Joseph has taken him away from us." Abby cried and a tear fell down Alex's face as he watched his mother cry.

Chapter 16

The journey back home took a toll on Abby. Her heart was broken and she just didn't know anymore. She saw her son with his father and he denied her again. Every time he denied her it got harder to bare. The tears continued to fall down her face like rain from a cloud. David couldn't say anything to her because he thought about how much his wife meant a lot to him and how much it hurt him to see her battling two cancers, Peter, the son whose pain ate at her body and regular cancer that ate away at her body. David glanced over at Abby, but she lay back with her eyes closed.

With each passing moment he noticed that his wife had not stirred, but gave it little thought. The closer he got to their home he gave into account that during the entire trip back home Abby slept facing the window and did not turn for a while. He knew that was her favorite way of sleeping, but something didn't feel right as he drove faster trying to get home.

A couple of years had passed by and Abby still hadn't heard from Peter. There wasn't a day that went by that she didn't think of him and his funny laugh, his pretty face, and how he fiddled with his ear. One day, she noticed that every month her bank account got bigger and bigger. She complained to the bank, but they had no explanation. They could only tell her a fake company was depositing money into her account. Deep down, she knew it was Peter. Every week she got strange phone calls and the person would just breathe in the phone, not saying a word. Abby would say, "Peter, is that you? I love you, baby, and always will." Then, the line would disconnect. Alex and David thought she was crazy.

Finally, Abby and David got married. He was so good to her and took care of her as his queen. Abby found true love and happiness, but she lost one of her sons so she wasn't completely happy.

Abby wasn't happy in Mississippi, so she moved to Indiana to be close to Peter. She hoped he stayed there after college and she could run into him one day. She dreamed of embracing her son and telling him how much she loved him. Peter had his own business. He started a software company and became a billionaire at a young age. He was married with two children.

A Family Divided by Color

Alex moved to Indiana, too, so he could protect his mother. Even though David was there, he still felt like it was his job to protect her. Alex had become a partner at St. Tosh Children's Hospital on 34th Street and he was a surgeon. Both of her sons filled their dreams to never live poor again. They both had big, beautiful homes, and nice cars.

Abby and David bought a house in Indiana after she sold the one in Mississippi. She and David had a small disagreement with that situation. He wanted his brother to live in the house just in case they came back, but Abby was against it. She said to sell the house because as long as Peter lived in Indiana that she would be there. She would stop at nothing to have her sons together again.

David sang at blues bars. He performed all the time, leaving Abby alone. It didn't matter because she had Alex, but her heart was empty. She and David had a daughter, Brooke, and she kept her busy most of the time. Even though Abby pretended to be happy, she kept praying to God for her family to be as one.

Chapter 17

Many times as a child he wished he could have gone to Mega Fun Time and now he is about to share the first time experience with his own kids. They arrive at Mega Fun Time the one place he didn't want to go because his mother didn't stay too far from there. Peter and his wife, Susan, had two kids, Jason and Michelle. Peter decided to take his family out to have a fun day. They did it on every Saturday whenever he wasn't busy with work.

They arrive at Mega Fun Time, Peter and Susan sat down on the bench and they ate while they watched the kids play. Susan noticed a glum look on Peter's face.

"Baby, what's wrong with you?"

"Nothing why?"

"You just look so down."

"It's nothing!"

"Are you sure? Because we can talk about it."

"I said it's nothing," he yelled as he slammed down his food and walked off.

Susan wondered what in the world had

gotten into him. She was tired of his mood swings and wished that Peter would just talk to her instead of going off, snapping on people. She watched him walk away and didn't understand why he got that way some times. It used to be every once in a while, but it became regular. She wanted to be there for her husband, but didn't know how.

She watched the kids and Peter returned to sit down. "I'm so sorry for snapping at you. Please, forgive me."

"Of course I do, honey."

They kissed and looked into each other's eyes.

"It's nice to see the children making new friends," Susan spoke.

Peter looked over at the kids and almost fainted.

"Peter, what's wrong?"

"Get the kids, let's go."

"Baby."

"Get the kids," he said as he pushed Susan in their direction.

Susan hurried over and gathered them as Peter looked over and tried to make sure that it wasn't his little sister, Brooke. And, it was her. Peter's family rushed toward him as Brooke looked over at them and wondered what was going on.

She ran over behind Peter's kids, Jason and Michelle.

He grabbed Susan by the arm and said, "Come on."

"What's going on? Who is that little girl?"

"Peter, let go of my arm. You're hurting me."

"Let's get out of here," Peter spoke as he continued to push Susan.

"What's wrong with you? Why are you acting like a maniac?" Susan questioned as Peter rushed her towards the car.

Brooke ran up to Peter and he pushed her down, then Susan reached down to pick her up, but Peter snatched Susan's arm and rushed off to the car. Brooke cried and yelled out, and Alex heard her.

"What's wrong, Brooke?"

"He pushed me down," Brooke cried as she pointed toward Peter.

"Who pushed you down baby girl?"

"That man over there," Brooke continued to say as she cried more.

Alex's face turned red and he ran off toward the car, but Peter got in and pulled off before Alex made it to them. He stopped running and stood there as the car sped off.

"Hey, you dirty bastard." Alex yelled

as he ran behind the car.

Brooked cried out and Alex rushed over to her. He gave her a hug and cradled her like a baby, protecting her.

"Baby girl, are you okay."

"Yes Alex."

"I'm sorry that bad man pushed you down. I won't let it happen again. You understand."

"Yes, Alex."

"I promise to never let anything like that happen again," Alex spoke as his memory went back to Peter jumping in his car like a little whimp.

He got more pissed as he thought about Peter and how he was just as rotten as his father. It was not the Peter that he knew. What in the hell happened to his brother? Who brainwashed him?

Peter looked back as Alex walked back into the building.

"Who are those people," Susan asked.

"Nobody!"

"What's wrong with you, pushing that little girl down? Have you lost your mind? You scared the kids to death."

119

"Damn, Susan, leave it alone," Peter snapped.

"Don't you dare talk to me like that in front of the kids?"

"I'm sorry. I don't know what came over me. I'm sorry."

"You should be apologizing to that little girl you pushed."

"I said that I was sorry. Either you forgive me or not, because I don't want to hear another word about it."

Susan looked at Peter. She has never seen him act like that. He acted like Joseph. She hated Joseph. Ever since he had been in Peter's life, Peter acted like a monster. She didn't like that side of him at all. He never talked to her any kind of way. She wondered who that little girl he pushed down was. She never knew Peter to abuse children. He was a loving and over protective father. *How could he be so cruel to this little girl?* she thought. Susan looked over at Peter and wondered what went through his mind.

As Peter looked out the window he felt very bad. That was his little sister he pushed down. He would never hurt at child, but that day he didn't know what came over him. It was a reflex and he wished that he could go back and apologize to her. Peter's thoughts brought tears to his eyes. A tear fell down his face and he looked up at the sky as if asking God for an answer. Why was it that he had a hard time coping with the stress? He wished things would get better. He knew that Susan was probably wondering has he lost his mind.

Chapter 18

Alex grabbed his cell phone and called Peter, but he didn't answer. The secretary gave him the number after flirting and talking with her one day. It took him about three days to get the number from her. After that day, he never spoke to her again. He hated the fact that he had to trick her, but he no other choice.

He was tired of Peter's bullshit. Somebody had to stop him because his mother had suffered enough. *When was all this going to stop*? he thought. He looked to the sky as if God would give him an answer.

"Lord, please place the love back into Peter's heart he has for us, especially my mother. She doesn't deserve to be treated like an outsider. Open his eyes and show him that Joseph means him no good. We love him Lord. Please bring Peter back to us one day. Please God, bring him back to us. Amen."

Alex flipped his cell phone open and dialed his mother. "Hello," a soft voice on the other end spoke.

"Hi beautiful. What are you doing?" Alex asked.

"Hello, baby. I'm relaxing today I don't feel well at all."

"Mama, what's wrong?" Alex asked while leaning against a brick wall.

"I feel weak and my old bones ache," she joked giving off a little giggle.

"Do you need me to come over?"

"You know you don't have to do that. David is taking good care of me. I'll be fine son." Abby replied as she gave a small cough.

"Well mama, I'm about to get off the phone. I just wanted to check on you." Alex spoke as he frowned up his face. He wanted to tell her what happened, but he didn't have the heart. She was already in pain.

"Okay baby. Just remember one day if you don't ever remember anything else. Remember that I love you dearly."

"I love you, too mama, always."

"Have you heard from your brother?" Abby sneaked in before Alex rushed off the phone.

"I've seen him around mama. Don't you worry about him? He will come to you when he's ready."

"I know son. I know." Abby said as

she hung up the phone.

Alex closed his cell phone and he closed his eyes while punching the brick wall. He wanted to kill Peter for causing their mama all of that pain. She did her best to hold them together as a family since Peter flipped out. Joseph would be the death of him. Alex hoped he opened his eyes before something tragic happen.

Peter looked at his cell phone and hit the ignore button. Alex called him again, but he knew it would be trouble if he answered. He couldn't believe that secretary of his gave out his cell number. Too bad he had to fire her.

Peter looked at his father and shook his head. He wanted to communicate with Alex, but his father thought it would be bad for his career. How could loving his family be bad for his career? He was raised as a Black man. And, his father wants him to be this racist White man that didn't like Blacks. He was torn and really didn't know which way to go.

"Why you looking like that," Joseph asked.

A Family Divided by Color

"I just don't understand you. How do you expect me to turn my back on my family?" Peter spoke with tears forming in his eyes.

"Son, you just don't understand. Those niggas are going to be the death of you. Watch what I tell you."

"Whatever? I'm getting so tired of all this mess you have created."
Joseph turned his nose up at Peter and turned his head. Peter put his head down. He had to stop that mess. What did his mother do to deserve it? He wanted to win his father's love, but not like that. It hurt him so bad to see the hurt in her face. He tried to avoid her every chance he could. Every day he looked in the mirror and wondered who that man was. He hated the person he become.

Alex rode around to look for Peter. He called his office and the secretary said he was out with his father. Peter couldn't believe how she just gave out the information. She didn't know if he was a killer or anything. Finally, Alex rode up on Joseph and Peter walking in the street. Alex slammed on brakes and jumped out his car in the middle of the street. The drivers honked their horns.

"Peter!" Alex yelled out.

Joseph and Peter stopped and turned around. Peter's face lit up, but he could see that Alex was very upset.

"What's gotten into you?"

"Alex…"

"He doesn't have to explain shit to you. Go away, boy," Joseph said.

"Boy? My name is Alex, not boy."

"I don't give a damn what your name is. Leave my son alone."

"Father, I can handle this," Peter said.

"I told you to do something or these niggas are going to ruin you," Joseph spoke.

"Father."

"What the hell you just call me?" Alex spoke angrily.

"I called you a fucking n…"

He didn't finish because Alex punched him in the nose. Joseph hit the ground hard. He fell down on the ground as blood came from his nose. Alex looked at Peter with his fists balled up.

"You really disappoint me. Joseph came into your life after you became rich. Mama doesn't care if you are rich or poor. She has always loved you and this is how you do her, Alex?"

"Don't fucking Alex me. I'm tired of seeing my mother hurt and crying herself to sleep at night all because of you. And, yes, I said *my* mama. I look into her eyes and I want to cry. She did everything she could for us and this is how you do her. I hate the fact you are my brother. You've did enough damage to our family. My mama loved you and you show no love in return. How sad you racist prick?" Alex remarked looking at Peter as if he wanted to punch him. Joseph got off the ground and Alex walked off.

"Just remember, Peter, God don't like ugly," Alex continued.

Alex jumped in this car and drove off. "Those people are your enemy," Joseph remarked. "Those people are my family. I was raised to be a strong, Black man and now, you want me to become this racist prick like you," Peter replied as he gave Joseph a mean look. He wanted to punch him in the jaw. Joseph has been nothing but trouble to him since the day in walked into his life.

He walked away from Joseph as he cleaned his nose and walked behind Peter. Alex was right. He could still see the hurt in his mother's eyes when they were younger.

She had this sad look in her face and he was reason why she cried. It hurt him to his heart knowing he caused so much pain to his mother.

Chapter 19

The sirens sounded off while they pulled in at the emergency exit. Alex walked outside after a hard day's work. It was three o'clock in the morning and his day started at 8 a.m. the previous day. Alex walking outside as the ambulance pulled in. Instead of Alex heading home, he ran up to the ambulance to help the EMT's. There was a child inside.

"What happened?" Alex asked in a panicky voice.

"We have a six year old child with 3rd degree burns all over his body. He's badly burned."

"Why didn't you all rush him to the burn center?"

"We were advised to bring him to the nearest hospital."

They rushed inside with the child and Alex helped as several doctors and nurses rushed to his side. Alex stood by and they rushed the child toward the back. He held his head down.

"Dr. Brenner, are you alright?" an EMT asked.

"I can't believe another child has been hurt like this."

"It was a house fire on 34th street and the child was trapped."

"Were there any adults?"

"Not that we could find."

"So, the child is alone?"

"For right now, he is alone."

Alex shook his head and walked off. He walked toward the parking garage. As he passed by a dark and musty alley, he saw a woman lying in the street yelling out for help. He got in a panic and rushed over to help her. As he ran past a blue and white dumpster, two men jumped out from behind and attacked him. One man hit him across the lower back with a baseball bat. Alex fell to his knees while the other man punched him in the face, knocking him to the ground. The woman jumped up and ran off into the dark alley.

As they beat Alex slowly, one of the men stated, "Stay away from Peter Brenner and his family. The next time you come around we will kill you and your family." They punched and kicked him until two nurses walked by and yelled out.

"Go get help!" one of the nurses yelled out to the other one.

A Family Divided by Color

The nurse rushed off to get some help. The two men jumped up, running. The other nurse rushed over to Alex. He lay helpless on the ground without a movement or sound.

People ran out of the hospital to go help Alex. He was unconscious, and they all thought he was dead.

Two of the doctors had sticks and they ran down the alley looking for the two guys that attacked Alex. A few more guys ran behind them to help, but there was no sight of them, the crooks ran off. So, they all returned to the hospital.

Alex was hospitalized with a few broken ribs, fractured leg, and a small concussion. Abby was by her son's side, praying and thanking God that he survived.

"Son, do you know who did this to you," Abby asked while placing a cold towel across Alex fore head.

"All I remember is this guy telling me to stay away from Peter and his family as he kicked me over and over."

"Oh my gosh," Abby whispered as she placed her hands over her mouth.

"Mama, I'm going to be fine. Just leave it to me. I'm going to handle Peter when I get out of this hospital," Alex threatened.

"No I will handle this. I don't want my sons fighting. I don't see Peter being involved in hurting you. This can't be possible."

"Believe it mama. This is not the same Peter you raised. This boy is a whole different person."

"Alex, I don't believe that he's changed like that. I raised you boys to be men. I will make him understand. He has got to understand."

"No mama. Promise me that you won't get involved in this. I will handle this myself. I believe that Peter and Joseph were involved. Say what you want to but Peter was involved," Alex spoke as he looked out the window.

"I have to make things right again. This is not how I raised my family. You boys were raised better than that," Abby spoke as she looked at Alex. She knew that Alex was hurt just as much as she was. She made up her mind to go to Peter. Something had to be done about all of that.

Chapter 20

Abby went to Peter's office because she was determined to find out the truth about what happened to Alex. He told her one of the men told him to stay away from Peter and his family. Abby walked past the secretary, who was on the phone and then she hung up.

"Ma'am, you can't go back there."

Abby kept walking like the lady didn't say anything. The secretary picked up the phone and called security. Abby walked by several offices until she found the right one. As she entered the office and everyone turned their heads to look at Abby. The secretary rushed up behind her and the small girl grabbed her arm, and Abby punched her in the nose. Her nose began to bleed and she fell to her knees as she cried.

"Are you crazy?" Abby yelled.

"Someone get security!" Peter barked.

"Have you lost your damn mind? Is it true that you had your brother almost beat to death? Boy, I didn't raise you to be an animal. I raised you better than that. You let Joseph come into your life and turn it upside down. What kind of monster has he created?"

"Where's security? Get her out of here."

"You don't need security. I'm leaving. Leave my kids alone. Don't make me come back. I won't be nothing nice the next time," Abby ordered.

Abby turned around and walked out. The secretary was still on the floor holding her nose while a brunette woman tried to help her.

"Excuse me, ma'am, are you Abby Brenner?"

"Yes, I am. Why?" Abby spoke angrily without a look in his direction.

"You don't remember me?" the old, gray haired man asked.

Abby looked up in his face, then her face went from a frown to a smile. "Mr. Hightower?"

"My Abby," he said while embracing her with a hug.

"It's so nice to see you," she spoke then looked back at Peter.

"I didn't know Peter Brenner was your son."

"Yes, sir, but according to him, I am nobody." She stated.

"Where's security? Get that lady out of here."

Abby looked back at Peter, "It was nice to see you again, sir." And, then she walked out of the office. Mr. Hightower looked at everyone in the office. By that time, everyone stared at Peter. Mr. Hightower shook his head, "I can't believe I was about to do business with you. Abby Brenner is a damn good woman," Mr. Hightower spoke as he walked out.

"Where are you all going? The meeting is not over," Peter remarked as if to ignore Mr. Hightower's comment.

An older woman stood up and spoke, "I don't want to do business with a man that treats his mother that way. You don't seem like that type of man, but I guess I was wrong."

"You should be ashamed of yourself," another older woman spoke.

Out of the twenty attending, only three people stayed. Peter stood there with his head down. He sat down in his chair, and then suddenly, he jumped up and ran out of the office. The few people that were left just stared at him. Peter rushed down the back staircase and caught up to Abby just as she was about to get in the yellow cab.

"Don't you ever come back here again," he spoke in a deep voice as he pointed his finger in her face.

"I am your mother and don't you dare threaten me," Abby yelled and slapped Peter's finger out of her face. She continued. "I raised you better than this. This monster you are showing me is just like your father when he beat me down and left me for dead. I was pregnant with you and he wanted us dead. You can pretend like he's the best father in the world, but I know better."

Peter stood there and stared into his mother's eyes. She reached out to caress Peter's face and he jumped back. Peter walked off and pointed his finger. "I'm warning you, old lady. Stay away from me."

I'm going to stay away from you, but you better stay away from my family, too. You're not the only one that knows people in high places." Abby threatened.

Abby looked at him until he disappeared inside the building. She jumped in her car and began to cry like a new born baby. Her son is lost. Alex was right. He was not the Peter she raised. Her son is lost forever.

Chapter 21

Peter drove his car as tears rolled down his face. He was at a red light when he beat on the steering wheel. "Lord, please forgive me. I love my mother. DAMN!" he yelled out. He looked up into the rearview mirror, "Peter, what's wrong with you?" He was very emotional, so he pulled over for a few minutes to get himself together before he continued home. He couldn't stop the tears from flowing down his face. He thought what in the hell is he doing to his mother. His heart weighed heavy as if he was about to have a heart attack. Peter held his chest and cried.

A few minutes after he had calmed down he laid his head back against the head rest and closed his eyes. A memory flashed before his eyes when his mother stood outside and played football with him. She taught him how to play football. His mother threw the football as if she had played the game before. He thought about her teaching him how to play basketball and to swim. She put her heart into everything she did when it came to him and Alex. But, the love he had for his father overpowered that. He wanted that father figure just like the other boy's he knew.

Peter shut off his thoughts and gathered himself to continue home. He loved his mother, but he loved his father more. Why was he torn between the two? Why they made him choose?

Finally, he arrived home. He cleaned up his face, got out of the car, and walked inside the house. As he opened the door, Susan sat on the stairway to wait for him.

"Hi baby," Peter spoke.

"Is it true that your mother is Black? You told me she was dead."

Peter held his head down without saying a word to Susan.

"Answer me!" she yelled.

"Susan."

"Don't Susan me! Do you know what this will do to my family? They will disown my children because they are Black. Answer me, god-dammit!"

"Yes, I do know, but no one has to know."

"So, she is Black? Well, too late for keeping secrets," Susan stated as she tossed a picture at him.

A Family Divided by Color

The picture landed on the floor. Peter picked up the picture and stared at it. It was a picture of his mother, Alex, and him when he was younger.

Susan stood at the top of the stairs staring down at Peter. "The kids and I are leaving."

"No, Susan," he sounded out in a low voice.

Peter stood there and stared at Susan as she disappeared into the bedroom. Suddenly, Joseph appears from the living room.

"I told you that nigga would destroy everything."

"I told you not to call my mother that, besides, you started all this mess."

"Well, I was young. Right now you need to make sure that Susan leaves and the kids stay. Don't let her take the kids."

"She's my wife. I want my family."

"We don't need her."

"We? There are no we in this."

Peter looked at his father and rushed upstairs to stop Susan. He entered the bedroom and Susan packed a suitcase while crying uncontrollably.

"Are you really leaving me?" he asked with disappointment in his face.

"Yes, my parents will disown me."

"It doesn't matter. We love each other. Please, don't go, Susan."

"I love you, baby, but I can't stay."

"I'm the same Peter Brenner you fell in love with."

Susan continued to pack as if Peter wasn't talking to her. She didn't care about what he said, she had to leave.

"I'm so sorry, Peter, I can't lose my parents."

"What about our marriage and our kids?" Peter asked while he fiddled with his ear.

"I'm sorry."

"Well, so be it then, you can leave, but you are not taking my kids."

"Peter."

"No, just get out. Remember, your parents would disown *my* children because they are Black. I see how you feel about your own children. I had to deal with the same bullshit and I vow that my kids will never go through that."

"Don't you dare talk about me not loving my children!"

"Get out! You are nothing but a money hungry bitch. Leave my kids and get out now. You want to go then so be it."

Peter picked up the suitcase and tossed it out the bedroom door. Susan cried, but he grabbed her by the arm and pushed her out of the bedroom. He picked up the suitcase and tossed it down the stairs. Then, he grabbed Susan by the arm and led her down the stairs in a hurry.

"Peter. Stop. You are hurting me."

"So, bitch. I see you never loved me. My father was right."

"Peter, please don't do this."

"Shut up! This is your choice," he yelled as he swung her around to face him.

They got to the bottom of the stairs and Joseph stared at them. Peter rushed over to the door as he held Susan's arm in a tight grip. He opened the door and shoved Susan out onto the ground. Peter picked up the suitcase and tossed it out on top of Susan. Susan jumped up and ran to the door, but he slammed the door and locked it.

"Damn you, Peter!"

"Go away. You left me, remember?" he spoke.

Susan continued to bang on the door as Peter leaned against it on his side. He couldn't believe she was the love of his life. He looked around to see his father who stood there with a smirk on his face. He laid his head back on the door and then Susan stopped banging. He stood there for a few minutes, and looked out the window.

Peter watched as Susan walked to her car with her suitcase as she cried. She jumped in the car and pulled off wildly.

Susan drove down the street with tears flowing down her face. Her thoughts were of Peter and how she loved him so much. She didn't want to leave him, but her parent's would disown her immediately. She couldn't leave her kids behind. What kind of mother would that make her out to be? She thought back to the hurt on Peter's face. Her obligation was to her husband and kid's, but how was she going to explain to her parent's that her family is Black.

Chapter 22

Abby was at the hospital by her son's side. When she first received the call about Alex being beat up she went into a panic. The doctors and nurses couldn't tell her anything over the phone. All she knew that he was hospitalized. Damn Peter if he was responsible for that mess. The good thing was that he was okay. His girlfriend, Xuxu, and their daughter, Alexis, were by his side as well.

"Guess what?" Xuxu said.

"What?"

"Alex and I have decided to get married. But, we haven't set a date yet."

"Oh my, congratulations," Abby said as she hugged Xuxu.

"I'm so excited. I hope you're up to helping me plan this big wedding."

"Big wedding? How big are you talking?" Abby asked.

"I don't know all the details yet, but I do know I want it to be big."

Abby looked at Alex and he looked like he wasn't happy. He had a glum look on his face and stared out the window as if he was lost. She knew that look, because she did it all the time when she missed Peter.

"What's going through your mind, baby?" Abby asked Alex.

"Nothing, mama."

"Boy, try again. I know when something is wrong with my child."

"Mama, I can't believe that Peter would have me beaten. Of all people, my brother. That is my family, my blood."

"Well, Alex, I don't believe that."

"That man stopped hitting me with that damn bat and said to stay away from Peter and his family."

"Watch your language."

"I'm sorry, mama. My own brother. My flesh and blood."

"It will be alright, Alex. I put it in the Lord's hand. He will take care of this."

"I know. But, my brother. My best friend."

Abby walked over and put her finger across Alex's mouth. "SSSsssshhhhh. It will be okay, baby. I don't believe Peter would do this. I raised him and I know better. I'm tired of all this mess. I will go see him today."

"No mama because if he hurt you, then

I will kill him."

"Don't talk like that! He's still your brother."

"Brother or no brother. If he lay a hand on you, then you are going to bury him. You can get your black dress ready." Alex threatened as he looked directly into Abby's face.

"Don't talk like that about your brother? God will work things out."

"I know God will, but if he hurts you. I'm going to kill him."

"You're talking nonsense, Alex. Things will work out. You just focus on getting yourself well and out this hospital."

"It's not nonsense mama. You need to wake up and smell the coffee. That boy is going to be the death of you."

Xuxu just stood back and stared into Alex face. She never saw him so angry and upset. Deep down, he was more hurt than angry. Abby took Alexis from Xuxu and placed a kiss on her jaw while she gave her a big hug. Alexis reached for Alex. Abby laid her in the bed with him. "I'm about to go home. Baby, do you need anything?" Abby asked.

"Yes, I do. A big hug and kiss from my mama."

Abby smiled. She kissed Alex on the forehead and tried to hug him. Alex hugged his mother and didn't want to let go. He loved her so much.

"Mama, please don't go visit Peter. I hate to hurt that boy."

"Alex, I have too. I have to put an end to all this drama."

"Please, mama. Please. Promise me."

"Baby, I can't promise you. I love you so much. I have to find out if he is behind this mess."

Abby kissed Xuxu and Alexis, and walked out.

"If he touches my mother, I will kill him. That's a promise," Alex said to Xuxu as he stared out the window again. He was tired of seeing his mama hurt and in pain every day because of Peter.

Chapter 23

Abby wanted to go to Peter, but instead, she went home. It hurt too much to think her sons would hurt each other. She prayed to God every night to have her family to be as one. Where did she go wrong? It seems like the more she prayed the worst her health became. She ached and ached all over. Abby could not sleep and nothing seemed to ease her mind. She would pray and that too caused her some form of grief. Her spirit told her that her time was coming to a close and she needed to prepare her family soon.

She prayed that she would hold on until things became better between her and her sons. Abby often look at herself and saw that she was nowhere near the same as she was when the cancer first got started in her body. Her hair comes out, her nice thick body was smaller and smaller by the months, and her appetite for life was almost gone. Her sons and David were the reason she lived and that too seemed to be fading away.

Days went by, and Abby thought about Peter constantly. He was heavy on her mind.

David and Abby lay in the bed together as he held her tight while she cried.

"Abby, forget about Peter. He will come around. Just keep praying and God will fix everything."

"I know, but I can't rest until I lay eyes on him."

"I know, baby. Just let him be. He can't hide forever. And, when he does come home, just be there with open arms."

"Oh, I will, because I have been through too much to just let my family go."

They lay together silently. Abby looked at David. "I went back to see Dr. Howard today and he gave me my test results."

"What did he say?" David asked as he rose up.

"I have cancer."

"No, Abby, you have what?"

"I have cancer."

"No baby. No. This can't be happening."

"Yes, David, it's true. I didn't want to say anything to you or my sons. Things are going to get better for me. God is not going to let me die because he knows I'm on a mission."

"Abby, how could you keep this from

me?"

"I didn't want you to hurt. I don't need symphony right now. I need my family to come together.

"Those boys are grown. You have to worry about yourself first."

"I know David, but my children are my world and I can't rest until my family is together as I raised them to be." Abby replied while staring at David.

While he stood up looking outside at the stars, he thought about how restful they seem to be. Each star was nestled tightly in its place and they shone ever so bright; however, it was not the stars that caught his attention. It was the way everything felt. The wind blew gentle breezes to the trees as it they were in a live conversation. The moon hung just right to emphasize how mighty the sky appeared to someone like him. His surroundings tried to shape him for the peace he knows he will need in life.

He sat there for a long time with his eyes closed and feeling the wind upon him. For some reason it gave him comfort and stabled his mind off how serious his wife illness was. His mid flowed back to her son, the one that she talked about all the time and how he didn't acknowledge her existence.

How can a child be so dumb? He thought, but quickly changed his thought before he got angry. David thought about his wife. Ever since he has been in her life she had never failed at a task. He further thought how she doesn't complain. He knew it was further than a stage one, but she kept trying to make him believe that it was just that and he let her think that he believes her.

The room was silent for a while. David embraced Abby as she cried herself to sleep. Later Abby woke up and vomited. She cried while she lay on the floor next to the toilet.

"Abby, please don't cry."

"You don't know my pain, David. I can't believe I have cancer. What about my children and you? How can this be?"

"Everything will be okay. We will survive through this."

"I'm losing my faith. What have I done to deserve this?"

"Nothing, Abby. You're a good wife and mother. You have done nothing wrong but love the people around you. You have a happy soul, baby."

"I'm not happy at all. I have a son that hates me and now I'm about to die."

"Don't you dare talk like that!"

"It's true. Face it because I'm dying."

David picked Abby up off the floor and hugged her tight. He held her like it was his last time. Abby had always been strong and at that moment she wanted to be weak.

"Abby, I love you so much. I promise that I will always be there for you."

"I love you, too, David. I'm face with so much and I don't think I can handle it. What am I doing wrong?"

"You aren't doing anything wrong. Stop saying that. Just keep doing what you are doing. Keep praying and have faith in God. God answers all prayers."

"I know David. It's so hard to keep faith when all of this is happening to me."

David kissed Abby on the forehead and led her back to bed. He placed her in the bed and pulled the covers over her. David turned off the lamp light and proceeded to bed.

After Abby fell asleep, David got up and went into the bathroom. He locked the door and sat down on the floor next to the sink. Tears fell down his face. He cried uncontrollably. David placed his hands over his mouth so Abby wouldn't hear because he didn't want to wake her. More tears fell down his face because reality was that his wife was dying. How could he face such a situation? He had to keep his faith. God had to listen to his prayer.

"My dear father, keep my wife safe. Take this cancer away from her. She doesn't deserve this pain. It's bad enough that she has to go through this with her sons. She's a fighter. I rebuke this cancer. Take it away and never return. Give it to me Lord. I'll take her burden. Just leave my wife alone and give me her cancer. I love her too much and I'm not ready to let go. Please Father, heal her. Amen."

The next morning, Abby lay in bed while not feeling well. David fixed breakfast for Brooke and took her to school. After that, he picked Alex up from the hospital.

"David, can you take me home?"

"Well, I really think you should go visit your mother today. She doesn't feel well. Plus, she has something to tell you."

"What is it?"

"I rather Abby tell you."

"Is something wrong with mama?"

"Yes."

"David, please tell me."

"There is only one way to say this. Your mother has cancer."

"She has what?"

"Your mother has cancer."

"Oh my God. Are you for real?"

"Yes."

"How long did they give her?" Alex asked as he almost lost his breath.

"I don't know she won't talk about it. I'm so scared of losing her. We have to stay prayed up and let the Lord know that this woman is needed here."

"She's not going to die. The doctors made a mistake," Alex spoke trying to convince himself.

Alex leaned back against the seat and stared out the window. He was hurt because his mother had cancer. All the questions develop in his head. *How long does she have to live? Can she get rid of the cancer? How long has she known about this? Has it spread all over her body?* So many questions.

They arrive and Alex went straight to the bedroom where his mother was. He sat down on the bed.

"Hi, baby. I see you look better."

"I feel better since I'm out of there. That food is whack. You know hospital food sucks."

Abby joked, "You should know. You work there."

Alex laughed, and then it disappeared. He lay down next to his mother and they looked up at the ceiling. The same way he and Peter had when he was hospitalized from the snake bite.

"Is it true that you have cancer?"

"Yes, baby, it's true. But, you know I'm strong. I will beat this thing."

"How long have you known about it?"

"It's been a while. The doctor said I can have it removed, but you never know."

"Well, I'm here to protect you and take care of you."

"I know, baby. You're always here to take care of me."

"Peter is so stupid by the way he's acting. I will never turn my back on you and the Lord knows I will put my life on that."

"Peter is a good boy, Alex, and you know this. He's just misunderstood and misguided right now. We have to pray for him, too." Abby spoke.

Abby and Alex talked for hours until they both fell asleep.

Two days had gone by and Abby felt better. She saw the doctor again and scheduled an appointment to have the cancer removed. The doctor wanted to move fast because he didn't want it to spread.

A Family Divided by Color

Abby left the doctor's office and drove home. She pulled in the driveway and sat there in the car for a few minutes. She held the steering wheel and she felt out of breath. Then, she sat back in the seat and relaxed. She had to calm down. Brooke was at school, David had gone back on the road to another one of his blues shows, and Alex had gone to clean his house. She thought of Peter. Why? Abby backed out of the driveway and headed over to Peter's house. She would see her son.

On her way over she thought about time to time, her and David would turn on the news and something about Peter would make front page, either he had created something or he was improving something that benefit millions of people. Whenever the report would go off she would always say to David "That's my baby, being famous as he said he would." She smiled as she thought back to all the newspaper clippings and magazines she had collected of Peter and his success. She smiled as she thought about when he was younger. All he talked about was becoming famous.

Chapter 24

Peter arrived at home from work early. As he pulled in the driveway, he noticed Susan's car. He jumped out of his car, praying that she came back home. He loved her and he wanted them to be together. He opened the door and Susan sat on the stairs with a puzzled look on her face. Peter walked in and she stood up.

"Peter, please forgive me."

"Why should I forgive a woman who turned her back on her family?" he asked.

"I was wrong for leaving my family behind. I love you and our children. There is nothing in this world that can take my family away from me, not even my parents. Please, forgive me for being stupid."

"You're not stupid, Susan, just confused. I know how you felt, but imagine me going through the same thing every day. One minute I'm being raised as a Black man, and then next thing I'm being taught to become a White man," Peter explained.

"I can't imagine how you feel Peter. Let's work through this and move forward. I love you no matter what color you are," Susan spoke.

"So what if I was green," Peter joked. Susan laughed as he ran to his wife and embraced her. She cried a few tears and he held her tight. They shared a passionate kiss, and Peter picked Susan up and carried her upstairs to make love to his wife.

He laid Susan on the bed while he kissed her. He took off his shirt as she helped him. Then, he pulled his pants off. Susan took off her pants and Peter opened her shirt and the buttons hit the floor. He caressed her breasts with his mouth. She reached down to caress his cock. It was hard and throbbing, she loved it when he was hard.

Peter took off Susan's thong and caresses her pearl tongue with his fingers. He couldn't hold back. Peter rammed Susan's pussy, making her gasp for air. He stroked very hard. She lifted her hips, making sure she felt every thrust. They stroked at each other until Peter exploded on her stomach.

Afterwards, he laid there and gasped for breath. Susan laid out as well until she saw that his cock was still rock hard. She jumped up and made his body call out for her.

Susan got on his cock and rode it like a cow girl. She rode him wildly like it was their first time. Peter flipped her off and put her in doggy style. He entered her pussy roughly and pumped until he exploded again. But, that time he didn't take it out.

They made love for the rest of the day until it was time for the kids to be picked up from school.

"Peter, where the hell are you?" Joseph yelled as he entered the house without knocking.

There was no answer, but he could hear the sounds from upstairs and he knew his son let that woman back into his life. He became furious because Peter was all his money and all. To disturb them he yelled a little louder, "Peter. Boy, you hear me calling you."

He was late they finished making love and were getting dressed. Minutes later Peter came down and answered, "Yes, dad, what is it?"

"What in the hell is going on with you

and Susan? Why is she here? Didn't I tell you that you don't need that woman? Don't you remember how she reacted to you being half Black?"

"She is my wife, and she lives here."

"You let that bitch back into your life after she left you?"

"Don't call her that, she's my wife. Have respect."

"Respect my ass."

"If you don't watch your mouth you will leave my home." Joseph threatened.

Susan came down the stairs and waved at Joseph as she walked out the door and left. Peter walked into the study as his father followed while shaking his head. He knew that making it where his wife could leave did not do the trick. Since Peter had been in his life he couldn't help it. Peter was smart and absolutely rich.   He had to think of ways to keep his son all to himself. Money ruled Joseph and he had greed in his heart. He didn't love Peter, but he loved his money and what legal tender Peter could bring his way. How would he get rid of Abby and Susan? Both of those bitches had his son's heart. He even had the thought of having them both killed. Then, he and his son could be   together   without   a   woman.

"Son, are you really going to let her come back into our lives?" Joseph asked him in a nicer tone.

"I love her and I hoped she would come back. The kids need their mother as much as I need her. From personal experience it is hard to be without love." Peter said as he remembered all the love his mother shown him even when he was horrible to her.

"Fine, let her back, but she will only throw it in your face about the other side of you, that you have tried to keep hidden for years," Joseph said as he walked to the study and puffed his pipe and began to think.

"You mean you tried to keep hidden." Peter smirked as he looked up at Joseph who gave him a look that could kill.

Chapter 25

Days had gone by and Abby was feeling like her old self again. She had to go see Peter because he hadn't come to her. Abby told David that she had to go to the hospital out of town for a couple of test and she didn't need him to go with her. He desired to go, but gave his wife her space and he knew she needed it.

Instead of going for test she pulled into Peter's driveway. Several cars and hesitated to go up to the door, but knew she had to do it because her time was at hand. She took a deep breath, and then went on up to the double doors. "Hello," Susan said as she stared into the woman's face. She knew immediately who she was. With more politeness she said, "What can I do for you, Ma am?" Susan asked as she answered the door. "Yes, I'm looking for Peter Brenner."

"Sure, come on in.

"What's your name?"

"I'm Abby Brenner."

"Oh okay, I take it that you are Peter's mother? I can see the resemblance in your face."

"Yes, ma'am, I am his mother."

They walked down the hallway when a door opened. Out stepped Peter and Joseph. Peter froze because she didn't look the same. His mother was older.

"What the hell are you doing here," Joseph yelled out before Peter could say anything.

Abby looked at Peter and asked, "Are you serious?" Then, she looked over at Joseph, "Are you the reason why my son is acting like the monster you are?"

"Your son?"

"Yes, my son. I raised him. Remember, you didn't want him. You turned your back on us when you got beat up, remember."

"Get your Black ass out of here," Joseph yelled out.

"Dad, stop it. Don't talk to her like that," Peter said.

"Peter, she's just another dumb nigga."

"Dad, don't call my mother that. I'm warning you," Peter said with so much anger.

"I will be whatever you want me to be, Joseph, but just remember one thing, you screwed me and now we have a son together."

Joseph leaped toward Abby and struck her across the face. Peter grabbed his father by the neck so fast and slammed him against the wall. "Don't you ever, ever in your life hit my mother again?"

"Get off me, boy. Don't you ever put your hands back on me or I'll kill you."

"What did you say?"

"Peter, no!" Susan called out.

Peter and Joseph stood toe to toe, looking into each other's eyes. Peter had enough of Joseph's mouth talking about his mother. He was one second away from busting his head open.

"Why are you here?" Peter said as he turned his attention to Abby.

"I want to know why are you doing all this, but I see that Joseph as a big part in this."

"Get out of here, nigga. He doesn't love your Black ass."

"Father!" Peter yelled as he grabbed Joseph by the collar and shoved him out the door. Abby and Susan stood to the side as Peter walked over to his father.

"You are throwing me out over her?"

"No, I asked you to stop disrespecting my mother," Peter stated as he slammed the door in Joseph's face.

Peter walked over to Abby. "Why are you here?"

"Is it true that you pushed Brooke down and put your brother in the hospital?"

"Alex is in the hospital?" Peter said with his mouth wide open.

"Yes, he got beat up by some strangers and they say you told them too."

Peter didn't answer. He looked toward the window watching as Joseph got in his car and drive off. He knew that Joseph was behind that mess, but he wasn't going to let his mother know. He didn't want to see the hurt in her eyes again.

"It's time for you to leave."

"I'm leaving, but, have you really lost your mind? I didn't raise you this way," Abby said as she coughed and coughed.

"But, since you deny me and your family, I will leave you alone from this day forward. Remember one thing; I have loved you since the time I found out I was pregnant with you. I didn't see color, I saw a child that needed his mother. You have denied your entire life. You have denied your brother who is your family and now since this is what you want, now leave mine alone."

A Family Divided by Color

Peter looked sad at Abby as she walked to the door. Susan held her head down. How could he be so stupid to act the way he did? That lady really loved Peter and he was so stuck on winning his father's love.

"Since you deny me, why don't you ask your father why he didn't want you?" Abby opened up the door and stepped out, but stopped. She looked back at Peter.

"Joseph said he didn't want you because he didn't want a coon as a son. I tried to shield you from this type of life, but you were so headstrong against me. I wanted you to see love and not color. I needed you to see that I loved you more than anything you could be, but you kept pushing me away. You kept denying me every chance you got. My heart breaks for you because I know you are better than what you are letting on. I don't know how long I have to be here, but I have said what I needed you to know." A tear fell down Abby's face as she looked directly into Peter's eyes. Tears slid down his face as well. She blew him a kiss and walked out. Peter fell to his knees crying like a new born baby as Susan held him.

Abby got in her car as she wiped her face. She had to give her worries over to God before it killed her. If Peter wanted to deny her, then so be it. She drove down Courtland Lane and headed back home. Alex would have been very upset if he knew she went by to visit Peter.

Abby drove and suddenly a car appeared behind her. It drove wildly. She waved for him to go around, but the car honked the horn and flashed the lights. Abby pulled her car to the side and noticed it was Joseph. He jumped out of his car and ran up to hers, and she let the window down.

"What the hell you want?" she yelled.

Joseph snatched the car door open and pulled Abby from the car by her hair.

"Get out, bitch."

"Joseph, stop."

He slammed Abby up against her car. She pushed and shoved him while she tried to get him off her, but Joseph had Abby by the collar of her shirt. She stopped squirming and stood as he pulled her collar tight. "Why do you keep hanging around Peter? He doesn't want you around and he doesn't love your Black ass."

"Did he tell you that?"

"No, I'm talking for him. Leave my son alone. I'm warning you this time. I should have killed your sorry ass years ago, but   I   didn't."

"You should have killed me. That's my son. Remember, you didn't want him. He's a coon, remember?" Abby spoke.

"A coon? You mean a nigger. The only difference is that he's a rich nigger."

"Get off me," Abby yelled as she snatched away from Joseph.

Two White women drove by and stared. Abby looked them in the eyes as if she asked for help. Suddenly, Joseph grabbed her face and turned her around. He put his mouth to her ear and spoke, "Leave my son alone. And, if you don't, I'd have to kill you. Or, I could arrange for your entire family to be killed."

"Joseph, don't do this. He's my son."

"Your son is dead. He's my son now."

"You only want his money and he's so blind to think you love him."

"Love him? Why in the fuck would I love a nigga?"

"You loved me."

"I loved you because you had some good pussy. I hope you didn't think I really loved you," Joseph bluntly spoke.

"You loved me Joseph. It's true I'm Black, but you loved me. I thought the loved we shared was inseparable, but you proved me wrong."

Joseph looked at Abby as if he could remember the love he once had for her. She looked into his eyes and could see that a little love was still there for her. She didn't know why he acted like he hated Black people and he really didn't. She loved him and he loved her once. The love was so unstoppable that they had a son together. How could he act like that?
"Fuck you, Abby," Joseph said as he pushed her in the face. Her head fell backwards, hitting the car. Abby grabbed the back of her head and looked at Joseph. "Stay away or I will kill you. I'm serious. Leave my son alone." Joseph threatened her as he walked away without looking back. He got into his car and drove off wildly. Abby stood there holding the back of her head.

A truck pulled up and two White women stopped to see if she needed help. One lady asked, "Ma'am, are you alright."
"Yes, ma'am, I am fine. Thank you," Abby spoke as she got into her car and drove off.

Joseph jumped in his car and drove off. He didn't realize how much he missed loving Abby until then. She spoke the truth. He was deeply in love with her, but his father put an end to the relationship. Abby had won his heart, but he became bitter over the years after Peter made millions and she tried to come between that. He didn't love Peter, but him money was another thing. If Abby didn't stand down he would be forced to remove her from the earth. He loved her once, but love money more.

Chapter 26

It was Saturday and Peter drove around town as he tried to get some peace with himself. He decided to go to the church and pray. It bothered him so bad that his mother wasn't in his life. It was true that he became a billionaire. He had money, but still wasn't happy. *How could he be happy*? Peter thought as he walked inside the church and looked up toward the huge statue of Jesus. He stared at the statue as he walked to the front of the church. Peter fell down to his knees and began to cry out for God and repentance.

"Lord, please forgive me of all my sins. I love my mother. Please, God, help me. I don't know what to do."

He stared at the statue for a few minutes, and then got up to sit down in the pews. He sat down, and then placed his head against the pew in front of him. He sat there for what seem like hours. Suddenly, he heard a voice, "Hello, Peter." Peter jumped up, looking around. Pastor Marlon Clark stood very tall.

"Hi Pastor Clark."

"I thought I heard your voice. Is anything bothering you?" Peter sat down on the pew and stared at the ground. He shook his head and did not say a word.

"If you don't feel like talking, it is okay. I will be here if you need me,"
Pastor Clark spoke as he walked off and Peter still said nothing, but something inside of him made him call after the preacher.

"No, Pastor, please stay. I need someone to talk to."

Pastor Clark sat down next to Peter. He knew something was really troubling him. "What's wrong, my child?"

"Pastor, I can't do it anymore. Sometimes, I think about taking my life. I want to die."

"Why death? I'm sure there's a better way to solve your problem. Tell me what's bothering you."

Before Peter could speak his voice began to tremble and his eyes became watery, "My mother has always shown me love, but she was the wrong color."

He looked at the Pastor for a reaction, but none was found. He looked at him, and then drops his head. He said, "She's Black and to be honest I don't see how she still loves me after all the denying I did to her and my brother. My entire life has been a lie after a lie or a cover up after a cover up. Whenever I could I would treat her badly and pray for her to leave me alone and now I may have that wish. She's in the hospital now about to die and I feel like I am the blame for her health."

"Peter everything is on God's time and you didn't do what you think you did to her health," The Pastor said.

"Pastor I have done nothing but stress her out and make her struggles harder than what they were. I was always displeased and never satisfied," Peter said as he cried.

"Peter, my child," The Pastor said as he placed his hands on Peter's back.

"Well, son, you can't win someone's love. Whoever it is; probably loves you and doesn't know how to show it."

"Pastor, to be honest, I don't believe that he loves me. He came into my life when I started making all of this money, so he's after money. He doesn't love me and he calls my mother these names. I hate it."

"I understand, son, but you can't make your father love you. Seems like he should already love you."

"Pastor Clark, he doesn't love me and

A Family Divided by Color

I know this. My mother has showed me so much love. But, my father says that by her being Black it would ruin me. I don't believe that anymore." Peter said as he lifted his head   up.

"You can't change the past. It matters right now what you do. You can't make up for lost time, but you can learn from it and go on. Go see her and ask her to forgive you. When she comes around show her that you love her more than ever. It is solely up to you. Now what do you believe you need to do?" Pastor Clark asked.

"I want to be happy. I love my mother so much, but I had spent almost all my life trying to win my father by denying my mother." Pastor Clark shook his head. He was about to speak, but Peter stopped him. "I thank you for listening, but I know what I have to do."

"I understand, Peter. Whatever your decision is feel good about it and, if you need me, I am here," Pastor Clark stated as he got up from the pew.

Peter laid his head down on the pew again and shook his head. Pastor Clark walked off, but he wanted to talk to Peter some more about his situation. He saw that Peter wanted to be alone, so he decided he would talk to him later.

As he sat there, Peter had a few memories. He thought about when he was ten years old. His mother told him about how people might pick at him because he was mixed. She explained it to him about racism, how many White people didn't like Black people and vice versa. She taught him to stay strong and never listen to people, especially if they talked about hate. He remembered that love has no color like the woman on the bus told him the first time he went off to see his father. The old White lady said "Love with color is not love at all." She was right. She never allowed him to feel inadequate to her or Alex. He opened his eyes and looked at the Jesus statue. Peter asked, "Help me, Lord. I don't know what to do." He closed his eyes and thought about more memories.

He thought about at the age of three years old, his mother and grandfather had a fight. They argued about something. Then he remembered, his grandfather told him about hate and race. His mother was furious and came after him. When she found him she hugged him so much. All he could remember crying and trying to cover himself with black ash so others would accept him, although his mother accepted him for what he was. His grandfather John hated White people and his father hated Black people, but it was his mother that loved both because he was both. She never chooses him over Alex or Alex over him.

His mother made no difference; even though, others made him feel the difference. He still remembered like it was yesterday as his mother sat on her recliner and how she told him that a mother has to protect her child from danger lurking all around, but she must protect me from my own race, my identity, and my own self destruction. *Oh, how she was right*, he thought as he sat on the church pew feeling like crap.

Peter shook his head while he tried to erase those memories, because he could remember his *I Can Be Me* book and how he loved to draw in it. He shook his head. Then, it hit him. His memory flashed to him graduating from high school and how he made a mockery out of his speech. After that how he went to college and never called, wrote, or visited her. He became completely devoted to his father and his cause. He remembered his mother said, "Peter, it will be tough out in the world, but remember that I love you and will do anything in the world

to protect you. That's what a mother does."
She continued to give him a speech on love
and family. He didn't want to hear what his
mom had to say and he couldn't wait until
she was finish because he was ready to go.

From that day on, he considered
himself to be White, and not as neutral like
his mother taught him. Peter stated to
himself, "I'm sorry, mama, but I will never
come back."

He opened his eyes and jumped up. He
was surprised by the slamming of the church
door. He had to get up. Those memories had
to be erased. He wanted his father to love
him all his life, had waited for so long to be
with him. Money held them together and he
didn't care. But, what made it so bad was he
had to lose his mother to win his father's
love.

As if a light was shining for the first time
in the darkness, Peter understood what he
needed to do. He knew it would not be as
easy as he hoped, but he knew what he had
to do, which was to deny his father and go to
his mother.

Chapter 27

Abby and David decided to have a family gathering. Abby cooked, but didn't feel well. When dinner was finished, everyone sat down to eat. Alex was there with Xuxu and Alexis, David's parents, Sylvie and Macon were there, and Abby's parents were there along with Brooke. Abby had all the family she needed with her. She missed Peter, but she gave it to God to bring him home.

Abby served turkey dressing, chicken dumplings, honey baked ham, stuffed turkey, cranberry sauce, chicken casserole, and many more delicious foods with an array of deserts. Abby didn't eat much because she ached all over.

She got up and began to feel dizzy, and her vision became blurred. She tried to grab onto the counter, but pulls down a cake while she was falling to the ground. David and Alex heard the sound and both jumped up and ran into the kitchen. David rushed through the door first, finding Abby laid out on the floor.

"Call 911!" David yelled out.

"Mama!" Alex called out.

Everyone rushed into the kitchen. Paula dialed 911 from her cell phone and Alex got down, feeling for a pulse.

"She's not breathing."

"Abby, no, please," David called out.

Alex did CPR on his mother until the ambulance arrived on scene. Five minutes had gone by and still no pulse. The EMT team rushed in and began CPR. Still, no pulse.

Later, Abby began to breathe. They had to put her on a breathing machine and she fought for her life. Abby had always been a fighter, so everyone knew she'd pull through.

"She has to be strong to pull out of this," the doctor told David and Alex.

"Abby's a fighter," David spoke.

Alex couldn't say a word. He couldn't believe that he was losing his mother like that. Not that way. He thought to himself that he couldn't lose his mother because she hadn't finished living her life yet. The family was not together as one. Who would he talk to everyday? His mother was like his best friend. He had already lost his brother, and then that happened to his mother. His world would come crumbling down if he lost the both of them.

Three days later and Abby was still not breathing on her own. She stopped breathing because her heart quit. Doctors thought it was a little strange and they expected the worst. They decided to go ahead and remove the cancer from her breast. Everything looked great, but Abby had to breathe on her own.

"I know this is a hard decision to make, but Ms. Abby isn't breathing on her own. Have you thought about the option of letting her go?" the doctor asked David.

"Hell no, we are not pulling the plug on my mother!" Alex yelled.

"But, Alex, we can't let her suffer like this."

"Hell no. David, why are you thinking this way? This is my mother, man. No way will I agree with this. No fucking way."

"Alex."

"No. I'm not killing my mother. She's a fighter. I know she will pull through this. I bet Peter will help her pull out of this."

"Peter is history," David spoke.

"No. You can't do this to my family. I have to tell Peter. I have to tell Peter about mama," Alex said as he walked away from David and the doctor.

"Just give them a little more time," the doctor said to David.

"I'm giving him time to tell his brother. I don't want her to suffer any more than she has too. She's been hurting for a long time and I know she doesn't want to hurt anymore.

"I understand," the doctor stated as he walked off.

Chapter 28

Alex knew that Peter would have a press conference that day producing new software. It's been announced on several news channels all week. He drove downtown while he hoped he could get in. He never saw so many reporters in his life. People were everywhere. Alex ran up behind the Channel 3 news crew and took a badge off one guy. They had so many people with them, and he walked right on in with them.

The press conference was about to begin. Everyone was standing around waiting on Peter to come out. Suddenly, the crowd seated as Peter stepped out on the stage. Alex was on the second row. He put his head down so Peter couldn't recognize him.

Peter gave his speech on a new software he invented dealing with creating Windows 4XZ for newer flat screen computers. He gave a short speech, and then was ready for the questions. The crowd was very aggressive. They seem very hungry to learn about the new technology.

Peter noticed a man sitting with his head down. He pointed out, "Next question, sir." He was pointing toward Alex. Alex stood up and Peter almost passed out. Joseph stood next to Peter.

"Security, somebody escorts that man out of the building," Joseph ordered.

"Mr. Brenner, is it true that you have a Black mother?" Alex asked.

"Sir, this is only about the new software product."

"Oh, I know, but is it true your mother is Black?" he asked again. He continued. "Is it true you deny you are Black? Did you have your brother beat down like a slave because you tried to win your father's love?" By that time, security had reached Alex and carried him out. "Did you know your mother is in the hospital dying? They about to pull the plug on her!" Alex yelled as they carried him out in a hurry. "Your own flesh and blood is dying. Your mother. You sick bastard, this is our mother."

Security opened the door and shoved Alex to the ground. He jumped back up and began yelling in the door, "This is our mother! What did she do wrong to you? This is our mother."

One of the big security guards shoved

A Family Divided by Color

Alex's head so hard that he went down to the ground and slammed the door. Alex got up and kicked the door. He screamed, "You bastard!"

Peter stood on the stage with tears on his face.

"Clean your face up, boy. Don't let that nigga ruin this for you," Joseph said in a low voice, trying not to be heard.

Peter shoved him. "This is my mother, you fucking cracker," Peter said angrily.

"Take your hands off me you fucking nigga," Joseph blurted out.

"Now your true colors show. I knew better than to think you loved me. It was all about my money. I turned my back on my mother for a father who doesn't give a damn about me," Peter spoke as he walked out. The press still yelled and screamed out questions.

Chapter 29

The secretary saw Peter drive up on his security monitor. She felt that it was either now or never for him to hear the truth. She stood by the door and knocked. When Mr. Joseph asked her to come in, she did, and left the door cracked enough for their voices to be heard. *Today, Peter will hear for himself*, she thought.

"Mr. Joseph, I have been working here for years and I need to know if I could ask you something, about Peter. I know you may not want to tell me, but I want to know?"

By her rambling she obtained his curiosity and he asked "What is it?" as he placed tobacco into his brown pipe.

"Is Peter a real Black man?"

He stared into her face, for some type of assurance of trust. She has been with the company for many years and she knew a lot of their secrets. He took a puff and thought, *Why not tell her?*

"He is a smart man," she said while he puffed, trying to give Peter time to hear the conversation and it worked.

A Family Divided by Color

At moment, Peter made it close to his office feeling like a new man. He no longer cared about his color for some reason. All he knew was he had to go see his mother. Going to the church did his heart well and he understood what he needed to do. The closer he got he noticed his father's door was cracked. The secretary saw him and with her hand waved for him to stop and listen. He didn't think anything of it, but the conversation got interesting when he heard the words.

"I swear that nigga boy of mine is stupid," his father said as he looked out the window office.

"How so?" the secretary asked.

"He lets that wife of his come back and those nigga relatives of his won't leave him alone."

"Susan is his wife and they do have children. As for his relatives they do love him don't they?" The secretary pointed out.

"I don't care a hoot about her, him, or those nigga kids of his. Over the years I had to intervene and make sure he never heard from them and so far it worked. Abby always sends him cards and she used to call, but since she been sick she waits on him. Awhile back I had to write her a letter from

Peter telling her he doesn't want anything to do with her."

He turns around, puffs his pipe, and laughed when he said, "That dam letter nearly killed the bitch. She had to be rushed to the hospital, but then she showed up here and I had to follow her. When I caught up with her, she and I had a few choice words she damn near died. Now, she is in the county hospital."

He turned around and said, "She is probably praying he comes see her, but he has so much animosity for Blacks and her, pride won't let him go. I know the White half of my son." He looked back out the huge office window and smokes.

"His mother is sick?" the secretary said in a sad tone.

"Yeah has been for years now, dying of cancer to be fact."

"That's sad, how long have you known?" the secretary asked.

Joseph turns around and looks at her then laughs a hearty laugh before responding, "Since Peter's been here. You know in business you have to keep up with what your opponent is doing and mine is almost out for the count," he said as he turned back towards the window.

"She's been sick that long? It's amazing that she is staying alive. What if he found out that you have kept him away from his family all because of your hatred for what some other people did to you?" the secretary asked as she looked at the tears in Peter's eyes.

"He won't do anything because he loves being White and so far has done everything in his power to make sure I am happy. Being White wins."

"Mr. Joseph, it's not about White, Isn't it about love?" she said compassionately.

"Love."

At the sound of that word he jerked around and looked at her as if she was crazy for saying such a word. Joseph took the pipe out of his mouth and says casually, "Fuck love, it only gets the weak weaker." He looked at her then puts out the pipe. Making his way back to the scene below he continues to admire the window view of the city. Then, he says in a meaningful tone of punishment. "He better keep making that money for me. If he don't he can go back to them. He should know that I don't love him, never had and because he is Black I never will."

"That is so cruel, Mr. Joseph after all

he has done to help you be some of what the man you are now," the secretary said.

She always knew the truth, but for some reason she felt that Peter needed to know for himself what kind of monster he called father.

"It may be cruel, but it's all about me. I'm sure if Abby had a job his life would have been better and he probably wouldn't have come to me, but I'm glad she struggled and sent the money making nigga my way."

"Mr. Joseph, don't you love him?" the secretary asked because she was being nosey and that was the main question Peter needed to hear.

"Hell no. The last nigga I loved almost got me killed. Ever since then I vowed to leave that kind alone," he said as he walked closer to the window as if he saw something.

"Let me get this straight," she asked to make sure she understood him correctly.

"You were in love with a Black woman?"

"Yes and I would have married her, but glad I didn't."

"You didn't try to help her when she was pregnant with your son?"

"He didn't become my son until I saw how White he looked and how naive he was."

"You didn't help her once he was born?"

"Why? When my dad made it hard for her, honestly he told her that she would pay. The nigga whore couldn't find a job so she had to move. She lost everything. She lived off her savings until she had none left. I didn't feel sorry for her because of what they did to me. Her house was run down, inadequate plumbing, holes in the floor, leaking roof, and her boys wore dirty clothes," Joseph said with laughter.

"You watched her struggle? You with all this money allowed your only son to live in poverty and endure pain?"

The secretary knew he was a real monster, but to actually hear how he did Peter and his mother she got angry.

"Didn't you see that Peter was White when he was born?"

"Yeah, but I had to make his life so bad, that way he would come to me on his own. Look it worked," he said as he held the pipe with his teeth and opened his arms to show off the fine office and all it had to in it.

"I played him like putty and I molded him to my fitting."

"If Peter leaves today, he will take the

company with him. Then, you will be broke with nothing."

"He isn't that smart. He loves me. Tomorrow I will be getting him to give me half the company back that way he would have to buy me out. Either way I will still be a rich man," Joseph said with pride.

"What about his brother?"

"He used to be a good kid, always tried to keep them together, but after that ass whipping they put on him the last time he was in this city, I am sure he will be leaving Peter and I alone. He should be glad that his injuries aren't as serious as they would have been if someone hadn't come and saw it."

"You had his brother beat up?" she said. She was afraid because she knew he help plotted an attempted murder on someone.

All he could do was laugh, and then he said "I plead the 5th."

The secretary decided that it was time for Peter to come in and she said,
"Huh Mr. Joseph, I think you need to turn around and look at this."

He turned around and saw Peter standing with tears in his eyes. To play it off he said, "Hello Peter, come on in."

The secretary eased out and she smiled

because she hoped that Peter put that evil hearted bastard in his place.

"All my life Joseph, I wanted nothing but to be accepted and love by you. And all my life you have done nothing in return but use me."

"Wait one damn minute, boy," Joseph said.

But Peter stopped him and said, "No you wait one dam minute and let me finish. I have bent over for you and now I am going to stand up to you. You turned me against the very people that have showed me nothing but love. They have always done their best for me and I repaid them by denying them. I am the biggest loser here and today I lose no more. You are fired and if you don't leave now, the police will be taking me to jail for killing you." Joseph was shocked. He never heard Peter talk to him like that and for years he ran Peter. He grabbed his jacket and Peter said, "Don't worry about the company it is mine. You still have your bank account, but your company spending and cards are all turned off. You are about to see how I felt growing up, knowing that someone had money, but had choose not to help me."

When Joseph walked out the secretary

went to Peter. "I'm sorry you had to hear that, but for some reason I felt you needed to know what kind of person you have been loyal too."

"Have I really been that naive to be blinded by color?" Peter asked.

"Well Mr. Brenner, you have been that naive. I just wish I could have told you sooner, but you wouldn't believe me."

"You are probably right," He said as he looked around the office.

She left him alone and he sat in the chair and cried for over an hour for being brainwashed and mislead by someone he assumed had his best interest at heart.

When he stopped crying he remembered his mother was in the hospital. He left the office and headed to his home to get his wife and kids.

That night, Peter lay in the bed thinking about what Alex told him. She was his mother, lying in the hospital dying, and all he could think about was his father telling him to leave her alone. This was the woman that raised him. She gave him the world, and he was being a disobedient child. How in the hell could he deny his mother? What the fuck had gotten into him? She showed him nothing but love, and this was how he repays her.

Peter was next to Susan and kept tossing and turning. Finally, Susan said, "Go to your mother. She loves you and you love her."

"I love my mother so deeply, and I can't believe I listen to my father."

"Your father is after money. You know it and I know it."

"Yes, baby, I know. I guess I just wanted him to be in my life."

"Go to your mother and tell her you love her."

Peter kissed Susan on the forehead and said, "I see why I fell in love with you. I love you so much."

"I love you, too, Peter. Go to your mother."

Peter jumped up, got dressed, and headed the hospital. As he walked up to the room, he saw Alex asleep in one chair and David asleep in another chair. He walked slowly up to the bed and his heart broke into pieces when he saw all those tubes in his mother. Tears fell down his face like a water faucet. He grabbed his mother's hand and bent over with his head up against her head.

"Mama, please forgive me. Forgive me. I love you so much. Please, don't leave me. I promise to stop." He tried to continue, but he cried out loud into her ear. David and Alex woke up, but neither one of them moved. Peter continued. "Mama, I promise to make it right. Please, don't leave me. You are my heart, my soul. Lord Jesus please forgive me. Our heart beat as one. I will never forgive myself for being so stupid. Mama, please wake up. Don't die, please wake up."

Peter continued to cry then suddenly, Abby squeezed his hand. He knew that his mother forgave him. Peter stood up all night long holding his mother's hand. Peter stayed until day break talking to Abby. "Mama, please don't leave me. I promise I will be back." He kissed Abby on the forehead and walked out.

Abby didn't have to strength to fight. She was tired. She had prayed long enough. It was time for her to go home to the Lord. She served her time on earth. There was one thing that held her back from entering God's Kingdom, and that was the fear of leaving her sons alone.

Lord, my true Savior, let me stay on earth just a little bit longer. My sons need me.

Chapter 30

When they arrived at the hospital, he was nervous and didn't know what to say. It had been years since he felt that way. He would reprove his behavior and show his mother that he loved her. As for his brother, he longed to become his best friend again.

Susan held his hand as they walked together ever so slowly. She had no idea how he truly felt, but she was there for him as long as he needed her to be. Susan took into account how quiet her children were. Somehow they too understood the importance of seeing their grandmother for the first time.

When they made it to the door, Peter stopped and held his emotions in his heart, for in there he was bursting over with guilt, love, and the desire to be forgiven. He looked at his family beside him, sighed, and opened the door.

Xuxu was there and she saw Peter and his family first. She didn't know them so she bump Alex's arm. He looked up and his mouth fell over. He stood up slowly and looked at him as if he couldn't believe that he was real. He smiled because it was his brother and he brought his family. Alex ran over to Peter and hugged him so hard. Words were not heard because the grown men were crying. David looked up and came over to them, but he did not bother them. He introduced the two families because the boys were finally embracing a hug that was long overdue. They finally stopped hugging and Alex walked Peter over to their mother and said softly in her ear, "Mama, I have a surprise for you. It's Peter and he has come to see you."

He watched for any sign of movement, but she did not move. Then, Alex moved out the way and let Peter speak into her ear. "Mother it's me, Peter," he said as he touched her ear because she knew that was his trademark. She moved some and Alex ran to get the doctor. He came and checked her, but told them it was probably her reflexes, but any sign was a good sign. And, not to read too much into the slightest things she does. He left out and Peter leaned back over to her. "Mother, please forgive me for denying you. I had been wrong as you tried to shield me from the pain I am now facing. I love you. Do you hear me? I love you," he said as he cried.

A Family Divided by Color

Alex grabs Peter by the shoulder and led him down the hall to an outside patio. They sat down and Alex said, "See how you came and she moved. That was the first movement she did since she closed her eyes."

"Alex please forgive me for not being a brother to you and denying you," Peter said between tears.

"Peter, I am just glad you came. It means a lot to me, but it'll mean more to momma when she finds out you are here."

"I have been lying my entire life about who I really am. Do you know how good it feels to finally feel free and not care what the color next to me is? I am finally experiencing the joy of life without trying to please people."

"I really don't know about you, but if you haven't noticed my wife is Japanese and they were like you except Xuxu and I were grown; therefore, it didn't get that bad for us. I hate that I didn't understand you like I should have, but I was young too. I mean I felt the same way, but I believed she loved you more because she was always trying to prove her love to you and not me."

"I am sorry for that," Peter said with a slight chuckle.

"I was kind of difficult to live with," Peter said as Alex laughed too.

"Difficult? You mean horrible. You remember the time we stole grandfather's truck and he was mad?"

Peter laughed and said, "I didn't expect you to run away with me, I thought you would have been happier if I left."

"If you had left, who could I complain to when things went real bad?"

"Look here," Alex said as he pointed to the spot where the snake had bit him.

They laughed and Peter said, "I can see the two dots a little. You were so brave. I believed you earned my respect that day because no one has ever showed me more courage than you did that day in the garden. I'll never forget that and to be honest I still thought about my life with you both from time to time."

"No. Do you remember when momma slapped you for running up in her face and telling her you were tired of her making us live like we did?"

Peter rubbed his jaw and said, "That was one of the hardest licks I have ever had in my life."

"We have had some times growing up the way we did. Look at us now. We have money, our own families and they are to be glad they didn't grow up like we did," Alex said as he looked at Peter.

For a moment they were quiet then Alex said as he cried, "It feels so good to have you back in my life. You don't have any idea how good it feels to have you here. To talk to you and to tell you I love you. To finally have my brother, my long lost brother, my best friend here."

They stood up, hugged, and cried again. It has been years since they shared a tender moment like that. It was clear to any on looker that they loved each other and how they were sincere.

Peter looked up and David looked at them. He came over and said, "Peter it means a lot to have you here. I called for the doctor because your mother squeezed my hand."

Without listening to the rest of David's sentence they both ran to their mother's side. As each of her sons got beside her they both held her hand and told her they loved her. In that moment, she squeezed both of their hands. They looked at each other and said, "She squeezed my hand."

They continued talking to her and rubbing her hand. The doctor came back in and stated, "It is truly an amazing thing, and how your mother is responding. That goes to show that God isn't finished with her."

"Yeah she always has been a fighter," Alex said.

"Not just a fighter, but courage, even when we didn't think it was there."

"How about love?"

When they heard that everyone looked around it was Abby and she was awake with tears in her eyes.

"Mama, you're awake. Thank you Lord Jesus," Alex spoke as he looked up at towards the ceiling.

"Yes, Thank you Lord," Peter remarked as well.

Abby spoke with a weaken voice, "Many years has gone by, but praying and praying for this moment has finally come. Thank you, Lord, for answering my prayers.

Epilogue

After Abby's recovery, her family was always together as one. Alex, Peter, and Abby were inseparable. Peter and Alex took their mother on expensive vacations anywhere in the world. There was nothing in the world that they wouldn't do for her. They both gave her whatever she desired.

Peter knew he couldn't make up for all those years he lost, but would die trying. He had disowned his father for down talking his mother and betraying him. Joseph tried to talk to Peter, but he refused. Abby told Peter to forgive Joseph. She said even though he was cruel and selfish, to forgive him. Abby told him that she forgave Joseph. Her family hated him, but she was raised to forgive and forget. She had learned to love all God's children.

Alex and his wife Xuxu added a son whom they named him Malcolm Alexander Brenner. Alex wanted him to be a Jr., but Xuxu disagreed. He bought a huge new house for his family and gave his old house to charity. He and Peter wanted to buy Abby one, but she refused. Abby wanted her home that she and David had built together. They worked hard to buy that house, and it was known as the family house. Abby thought that when they had family gatherings, her children had to have somewhere to go, especially her grandchildren.

David continued to sing every once in a while whenever Abby could get out because he didn't want to leave her alone. Someone was always by her side. He ended up being a famous blues singer with three albums out.

Alex and Peter were inseparable. They were like two peas in a pod all over again. They were two brothers joined together again by the love and faith of their mother. Abby had to go through trials and tribulations to get her family back together, but it paid off in the end.

Three years passed and the cancer came back stronger than ever. Abby lived her life and was ready to rest. God had called her home to His kingdom. Abby died at the age of 49 years old, and she got to know all her grandchildren before she passed. But, before she died, God answered her prayers. She reunited her children to be together as one, A FAMILY!

Amanda Lee is one of many authors at Vicious Ink Publications in Mississippi. She lives in Madison, Mississippi with her husband, Michael, and daughter. She became interested in writing at the age of sixteen while attending school at Sebastopol High School. It was that moment on that her family and friends knew she would become one of the best writers around.

Made in the USA
Charleston, SC
02 May 2013